A PRIVATE MAN

Stephanie Sy-Quia's first book of poetry, *Amnion*, won the 2021 Forward Prize for Best First Collection, an Eric Gregory Award, and a Somerset Maugham Award. It was longlisted for the Rathbones Folio Prize, the Laurel Prize and the Royal Society of Literature's Ondaatje Prize. Her writing has appeared in the *Financial Times*, *The Guardian*, *The Boston Review*, *The White Review*, *Five Dials* and *Granta*, among others. She lives in London.

STEPHANIE SY-QUIA

A Private Man

PICADOR

First published 2026 by Picador
an imprint of Pan Macmillan
The Smithson, 6 Briset Street, London ECIM 5NR
EU representative: Macmillan Publishers Ireland Ltd, 1st Floor,
The Liffey Trust Centre, 117–126 Sheriff Street Upper,
Dublin 1 DOI YC43
Associated companies throughout the world

ISBN 978-1-0350-5261-5 HB
ISBN 978-1-0350-5262-2 TPB

Copyright © Stephanie Sy-Quia 2026

The right of Stephanie Sy-Quia to be identified as the
author of this work has been asserted in accordance with
the Copyright, Designs and Patents Act 1988.

The quote on p. 270 is from *The Pearl* by Simon Armitage, Faber & Faber

'The Night/2', from *The Book of Embraces* by Eduardo Galeano, translated by
Cedric Belfrage w/Mark Schafer. Copyright © 1989 by Eduardo
Galeano. English translation copyright © 1991 by
Cedric Belfrage. Used by permission of the author
and W. W. Norton & Company, Inc.

All rights reserved. No part of this publication may be reproduced, stored in
a retrieval system, or transmitted, in any form, or by any means (including,
without limitation, electronic, mechanical, photocopying, recording or
otherwise) without the prior written permission of the publisher.

Pan Macmillan does not have any control over, or any responsibility for,
any author or third-party websites (including, without limitation, URLs,
emails and QR codes) referred to in or on this book.

3 5 7 9 8 6 4 2

A CIP catalogue record for this book is available from the British Library.

Typeset in 11.5/15pt Adobe Caslon Pro by Six Red Marbles UK, Thetford, Norfolk
Printed and bound in the UK using 100% Renewable Electricity by CPI Group (UK) Ltd

This book is sold subject to the condition that it shall not, by way of
trade or otherwise, be lent, hired out, or otherwise circulated without
the publisher's prior consent in any form of binding or cover other than
that in which it is published and without a similar condition including this
condition being imposed on the subsequent purchaser. The publisher does not
authorize the use or reproduction of any part of this book in any manner
for the purpose of training artificial intelligence technologies or systems.
The publisher expressly reserves this book from the Text and Data Mining
exception in accordance with Article 4(3) of the European Union
Digital Single Market Directive 2019/790.

Visit **www.picador.com** to read more about
all our books and to buy them.

For my mother

Woman, unclothe me, undoubt me.

– Eduardo Galeano, *The Book of Embraces*,
trans. Cedric Belfrage

Contents

Prologue   1

Part I   5

Part II   125

Prologue

2018

They put the neat box into a crisp hole in the ground. Everyone filed past to look down on it and throw roses in. Adrian felt dizzy, standing there, at the cut edge of the earth.

There was a knotted old yew tree, just as he'd been told there would be in any English churchyard. The gravestones came out of the ground like fungal nails. The church was small and dark and damp, bevelled with mossy flint.

He stood awkwardly at the edge of the car park, trying to see who he could name from the last gathering of the clan – his grandmother's phrase – but nothing came. His mother's genes were patent, playing out in the planes of the women's faces. He recalled the family anecdote of his mother, aged sixteen, walking into the local pub, and being greeted by the person behind the bar: '*You're* a Fletcher.' She was. And he, Adrian, was Hilary Fletcher's only son.

Adrian couldn't remember his grandfather; he'd died of cancer when Adrian was four. There were only images: a plate of grapefruit, strong black coffee, knocking at his grandfather's door with a tray, the giant pink pills in the packet that his mother waved in front of him saying never,

ever take these, even if they look like sweets; the arrival of all these relatives he didn't know, whom he stood near to now, not quite among. David Fletcher had long gone to ash, and this was his brother Ralph's funeral. A wintertime bout of pneumonia. He'd been nearly ninety.

The coffin had come in on the shoulders of Ralph's sons and his sons-in-law.

When the priest began to speak, or when members of the family stood up to read from the Bible, Adrian found he could not listen. His mind relinquished the rhythms of it. He stood for the singing and hid his voice among the others.

At the wake, held at the local golf club, his mother's eldest cousin, Emma, pulled him aside. He made excuses for his mother not being able to make the trip from California but Emma batted them aside. She had been corresponding with his mother about a crucifix, she said; had Hilary told him? She had not. It had belonged to his grandfather, David, apparently, but when he had died, Hilary had given it to Ralph, and now Emma had asked if she wanted it back. She did. Emma brought Adrian into a side room. The crucifix was larger than he was expecting, about forty centimetres. Emma unwound it from its bubble wrap to show him. The cross was made of ebony and the statuette of ivory. The Jesus had an intricate curled beard, and the muscles of his abdomen glistened into the drape of the loincloth. The nails pressed into his palms like mattress buttons.

Emma showed him the note she'd typed up to show to Customs. For the ivory, she said. If they ask. The note stated that the crucifix had been won by Adrian's great-grandmother as a school prize in Douai, circa 1913.

– All right, thank you, Adrian said. But why didn't Mum want to keep it, when Gung died?

Gung had been a name of his own devising.

– Oh I don't know, said Emma. He could see her attention being drawn to the washing-up her sisters were already coordinating in the kitchen. – I imagine that after . . . everything that happened, your mother didn't want anything to do with all of that stuff.

– What do you mean? What stuff?

– Oh you know. She was matronly now, brisk. – The laicization and all that.

– What's that?

The Fletcher sisters had formed an assembly line, and the brothers, all men in middle age, were queuing up to hand their dirty dishes over the counter.

Emma pivoted back to him.

– What's that word you just said? he asked again. What does it mean?

Emma looked him up and down, and then the plough line disappeared from between her eyes and her face flashed wide and open.

He googled it in the toilets.

Knowledge like a cord cutting.

He tried to call his mother, but the time difference was off. Only dawn in California. He was angry, embarrassed, already a little drunk. He went outside to stand in the undercroft of the clubhouse, staring out at the rain.

His grandfather had been a Catholic priest: a short story in ten words or fewer. And him the living proof.

PART I

1

1953

A LESSER SQUARE in Rome. The hour of the Angelus was near, when all the city's bells would ring together, all at once and out of time.

Ambient city sounds: fountains, footsteps, pigeons, shutters clapping closed, the distant clatter of cutlery on marble cafe tabletops.

There is a church. Its tall doors are open. Inside: movement, many figures clad in black. A white figure approaches from the dark. It does not step into the light: a man, surplice pleating and re-pleating as he walks. He reaches up and shuts the doors.

Within. The sound of a match being struck: the lighting of the frankincense. The tiny crystals catching, the latching of the silver lid closing over them. The thurible begins to swing in its chains; the incense dispensing itself. A moment more of chiselled silence, then the organ starts up, hard and base. The creak of a pew. The singing begins: male voices, some kind of introitus. Row upon row of women in black, their backs. This is the left side of the church, where the women sit. Some of them are fanning themselves. (It is June.) Their shoes are polished many times, creased where bunions are, and sensible. Their ankles are crossed. Their hands are in their laps (some twisting their rings, a few with high solitaire diamonds sitting proud on their fingers), their faces under black lace veils. These are the mothers. They vary in age. All are somehow identifiably English. Some of them whisper. The mothers have been smiling at one another timidly, sometimes shaking hands. Some of them have discovered they have sons who know each other, recognizing surnames mentioned in letters home. Others have met neighbours who live in adjoining parishes – places locally famed for the priest holes in particularly tenacious nobles' stately homes, or for churches where frescoes have lately been uncovered after centuries, protected in haste as the King's troops marched north. These women are offering their (sometimes eldest, sometimes only) sons to the priesthood. These women met and recognized this kinship like the flicker of a pilot light.

Outside, the diegetic music mutes.

Back inside the church: Claire Fletcher seeks a reassuring glance from her husband, Edwin, across the aisle. He lifts two fingers to his lips in answer, and leaves them lingering there. Her husband: that kind, good man who had submitted to the font for the love of her. Those hands which had held the heads of her sons; which had knocked on her father's house in the last year of their teens, when the roses were acraze over the grey stone of the door; which had pulled her to him all the best nights of her life, into that form of secret, sacred praise. He looked on in a state of well-meaning partial comprehension. The painted saints gazed back.

Then the organ music, elemental and sounding from some

dark blood-deep, groaning above the door – parting now, letting in the light to hit the frankincensy dim – and in they come. They number about a hundred: men, young, chasubles rolled and pinned at the shoulders, wearing white robes with hems of bride-like lace, lining up before the altar. There is David, and the one who stands beside him, and all the others behind. Their hands are clasped before them now. The organ gives a strange sonorous whinge again. They process, fanning out at the top of the aisle. Their robes all differ slightly from one another.

Claire shifts subtly in her seat. She catches the eye of the mother next to her and smiles. The other mother smiles back. The seminarians prostrate themselves in rows.

Claire stood at the foot of her son's bed. She had sewn his name into every piece of clothing he owned. The new cotton jersey underpants ordered from the catalogue in two different sizes, 8–10 years and 10–12 – he was growing so quickly now that she couldn't trust they would last a whole term. She had asked him laughingly where would be most comfortable to have a label and he had given it great thought. The neat flannel pyjamas and the little dressing gown. Things that were not clothes: his bedding, the blond-wood comb, the washbag, the shoe-polishing kit in the leather case. She stood over the trunk, and let a finger linger on the stacks of things new, freshly washed, and soft. All that would soon be touching his skin. She drew her hand back up towards her body, and as it went it passed through an imaginary cupping of his head. Her hand came to rest on her stomach, which puffed now with the memory of her children's passage.

There was a knock at the door. Maisie appeared to tell her the car was outside. She nodded and snapped the trunk shut. Its clasps made a pleasingly solemn clicking sound. Outside on the gravel, the car waited, deep blue and freshly buffed. At its wheel was her husband, and on its back seat was David, his hair combed badly, wearing his new navy coat. In the boot was the black tuck box with its large brass studs, the cake tin secreted inside, and Maisie, with the help of John, was lowering the trunk in alongside it.

Claire opened the car door and slid in next to Edwin. They both turned to wave to Maisie, standing on the step. Edwin pulled the car out, the gravel popping beneath it.

David slept for most of the drive, and Claire's hand rested on Edwin's knee. As they approached the school grounds, they joined a long convoy of cars similarly populated with groups of three or more, small blond and brown heads bobbing on back seats, visible through rear windows. The gates were enormous and toothy, painted a high-shine black. They opened onto a long straight drive, wide as a shooting range, with clear lines of sight up to the main building. It was a fussy, turreted thing, one of the less-commendable excesses of the Gothic Revival. It contained a mix of influences: a lead-and-clapboard-covered turret stood at the centre of the roof, at odds with the two pointed ones which rose up on either side of the door. The windows in their thick stone frames were tall and narrow, and the gables were made of ugly stripes of red brick and limestone. This was the place she must leave him to. She knew how it had gone with her brothers, sent to Ampleforth. They came home with new cruelty in their humour, and shied from their mother's touch.

The cars were discharging mothers and boys. The boys wore, inevitably, their new uniforms, which were all too big. Some, like David, also wore their coats. All had bare legs, knees no doubt recently daubed with damp cloths for scratches or mud or grass stains; all wore neat shiny shoes. The more eager wore the striped school hats already.

– Are you ready, darling? Claire reached for David's hand but he did not take it. He gave a small squaring of the shoulders and then walked in ahead of her. A woman with a pinched look was standing just inside with a clipboard, greeting all the parents. She looked down at David with a demonstrative smile.

– Good afternoon, young man! And you are?

– David Fletcher, miss. That's my mother. His pink finger pointing. Claire told him not to.

– Ah, Master Fletcher. The woman's pencil moving down the columns of names. You're in B Block, bed fifty-two. Straight down this corridor, third door on your right. Claire watched as the woman's eyes flicked from David's forehead to herself and Edwin, stood behind him. – Mr and Mrs Fletcher? Try to be brief. We like to give the boys five minutes to say goodbye.

He was off already, walking quickly, swinging his arms a little artificially, something in him hardened. Had she already passed the last time, Claire paused to ask herself, that he would ever hold her hand? She pushed the thought away abruptly. This was the way of it: your children were yours until they were eight. Then they needed to be sent away to become something else.

It was a necessary rupture.

This idea required a certain level of investment from all of them.

All around them the scene was repeating itself: boys were pulling ahead from their parents like competitors in a walking race, moved by the desperate need not to cry. Mothers kept up with their offspring, eyeing each other subtly, clasping handbags, brooches glinting on the lapels of their suits, some, like Claire, having travelled for hours in their good shoes which rubbed.

They took the third turn on their right, passing classrooms with mullioned windows and a dining hall with a high ceiling and chairs stacked against the walls, and came into a long room, the length of a boathouse, with thin diamond-leaded panes. More of that black paint on the window traps. Beneath them, the cots: narrow and metal and white, with sheets austerely tucked around the mattress on all sides. Each bed was high enough to accommodate the tuck box and the trunk beneath it. Each one had beside it a small chest of drawers and a narrow wardrobe. That was it. The modular configuration, perfectly smoothed and sparse, went on and on until the end of the room, some sixty beds.

David faltered, his pace slowing as he made his way into the room, and Claire watched him, fighting the ache growing in her chest. She stood beside him, her hand hovering above his lower arm.

– That's right, darling (at the 'darling' he bristled visibly, and Claire's breath caught in her throat), bed fifty-two. It was on their right, a few beds away. David walked to it and stood at its foot, looking at his shoes. There was a pause. Claire went to him and suddenly his steely resolve melted; he leant into her, rubbing his head on the tweed of her jacket, his chin puckering like the skin of an orange.

She and Edwin sat down on the bed on either side of him, facing away from the other boys filtering into the room. They took it in turns to stroke his back. He said nothing. Then: I miss Ralph.

– I know you do, said Edwin. But you will only be here without him for a year, and then he'll come and join you. So you need to make sure that you've learnt all the tricks here before he does, don't you? We wouldn't want him turning up and having his big brother not being able to show him the ropes now, would we? David looked up and gave a grave nod. With that they got up, Edwin reached out his hand and David shook it seriously. Claire permitted herself to reach out and smooth his small lapel, and they left.

The mothers were being called up to receive communion from their sons now, the final part of the ceremony, and their first act as newly anointed priests. Already Claire's row was emptying, and she shuffled along to join the others and form a queue. Inside her body, the hammerbeams of her heart pulsed hot with song. Here was her son. Her first, whose first finned movement she had felt gardening, so soon after her marriage. Her son whom, to her and her husband's happy surprise, had turned out to be a man of staggering beauty, the profile that of a demigod on a medallion, lips like Antinous's in the Louvre. She knelt before him, and he winked at her. Slowly she lifted her veil, brought her hands together, opened her mouth, received the host from his hand, took the cup.

Bells again. Doors open. The fresh priests filed back past,

and out into the square and its sun. Immediately, they began dabbing at their brows surreptitiously with their sleeves. The mothers walked on, stopping to link arms with their husbands as they did so.

David had never felt so beautiful, there amongst the newly anointed, these men beside him, under the blue sky and the ruthless light of Rome, the beginning, the end, the threshold.

2

CHATTER IN THE square. Pictures are being taken. The bright white-robed men kiss their mothers, who, delighted, receive. They walk together, a loose pack, to the Venerabile.

From the street the seminary looks like a grand townhouse, and in essence it is. The chapel has a modest, mock-Romanesque facade that runs along one half of the frontage on the Via di Monserrato. It is rectangular, with a timber ceiling painted in shades of olive, ochre, rust. The side aisles feature groin vaults, painted blue and punctuated with gold stars, and the gold-topped marble Corinthian columns hold them up.

Past the chapel is the dining room: small, with windows out onto the courtyard garden. The tables are round, with cloths of butter-yellow damask. On the ceiling is a painting of St George slaying the dragon – college legend has it that there had been some squabble over the painter's fee, so he had given George's horse farcically large balls, and condemned the seminarians to eat under them as long as the plaster held out. David and his peers had obliged, making many jokes, and the staff had rolled their eyes at them good-naturedly.

The garden is a treasure of the college: tight beds of roses and lavender, and herbs under the windows of the refectory and the kitchen which border it. Along the outside wall of the second chapel is the azure lozenge of the swimming pool. This was a precious, semi-secret asset: affectionately named 'the tank', it had been classed as a water storage tank so that the municipality wouldn't decree it an unfair frivolity during heatwaves, and force the college to drain it.

It is into the garden that they walk now, where tables have been laid out for them, ranked with Prosecco, glasses, great tubs of ice. There are crostini, olives green and black, seasoned with crushed garlic or salted lemon, or herbs and sweet red peppers; there are tiny Yorkshire puddings piped with horseradish cream and overlaid with pink petals of roast beef; cheese and crackers from tins, row upon row of minuscule sausage rolls, and cherry tomatoes individually impaled on toothpicks with cheese. There is more exotic fare, too, which David's father sets about sampling quizzically: arancini (a reaction of pleased confusion), anchovies on coracles of toast, huge silver bowls of stone fruit and grapes. Cherries glossy as horses' haunches and pert wild strawberries with their green ruffs. Pot-bellied jugs of cream. A Victoria sponge oozing seedy raspberry jam on a high stand. Smoked trout, frilled with half-moons of lemon, already being hacked at inelegantly by guests. The parents paired off, or stood around in groups, talking about home, or their forays into the sights of the city.

The other members of David's cohort were clapping each other on the back, calling each other by their last names enthusiastically, asking about future plans and postings. David put a cherry in his mouth and pulled the stalk off with a pop. A hand clapped on his own shoulder startled him, and he spat the stone out into his palm, where it left a crimson ghost.

– Fletcher!

It was Taylor. David answered some questions about where he was being posted; promised, when entreated to do so, to stay in touch. The others were laughing loudly; Malcolm was zealously topping up everyone's glasses.

A short speech was given, and glasses raised. Something rousing about a bright Catholic future, reference to several of this graduating year having served in the war, a commendation of their valour. There was a joke made – rather daring, David thought – about the second Elizabeth's attitude to them, as opposed to the first. (She, Elizabeth I, had hung, drawn and quartered some forty-four seminarians upon their return to England. These were known as the martyrs.) The speech concluded, as David imagined it did every year, with a quotation from the martyrs' painting in the chapel: *Ignem veni mittere in terram*. I bring fire to the earth.

– Now I invite you all, my new brothers, to make all final preparations for your departure. Parents and guardians, thank you for the support you have shown today, and always, in bringing us this most promising crop of new priests. We are for ever in your debt and service.

A sonorous 'Hear, hear!'. Glasses raised again. His mother at his elbow. – We'll see you for dinner, darling. The crowd in the courtyard thinned out. Many of the seminarians went upstairs to their rooms, to pack and change. David made his way in that direction. The first leg of the staircase was dark, but after the turn it opened up from the light of the first-floor loggia. The seminarians' double rooms faced onto this, across three floors – room for eighty students, all in all. As David walked along the corridor, he saw his peers folding their clothes, their suitcases open on their beds, or friends embracing. A few doors fell to as he passed, kicked closed.

– Are you coming back downstairs, Fletcher? It was Jameson, in his swim shorts, his towel over one shoulder.

David smiled yes. He continued on to his room.

Once inside, he pulled his robes over his head, undid the long flank of covered buttons on his cassock, and stepped out of his shoes. Underneath he wore an undershirt and plain cotton boxers.

He was naked with himself for a moment, and looked in the mirror. Then he broke his own gaze and stepped into his swim shorts, which were cobalt blue, picked up a towel from the fresh ones stacked in tight rolls at the end of the bed, and retrieved his sunglasses.

Back downstairs, the pool was thrashing with activity. Taylor and co. were sipping Old Fashioneds, hooked onto the pool's edge with their elbows, and Jameson was practising his butterfly, the muscles of his back Mannerist with the effort. David made for a lemon-coloured sun lounger, flinging his towel over it. He let his sunglasses fall down over his eyes. Malcolm, who lay on the next one over, had his leg in the air, applying oil to the back of his knee. Carter lay on the third lounger along, his eyes closed to the full sun, his taut chest already misted with sweat. Someone pressed a cold drink into David's hand, and he drank it gratefully. Others were swiping the remaining bottles of Prosecco and bringing them over to the edge of the pool, to swing their legs in the water slowly. Pleasantries were batted lazily back and forth like shuttlecocks; the laughter was raucous and then mellowed. They had this last afternoon together, to splash here for a time, to exalt in this feeling of their own new-mintedness. This was the last time they would be together like this, their hairlines firm and their complexions clean. They were all called David or Charles or James or John.

They had had the run of Rome together, for a time. They weren't allowed out unless they were wearing their cassocks, which they called 'the rig'. They dared one another to walk the streets naked beneath them, and as the heat crept up in the spring, the breeze on an ankle became a cherished pleasure. When the summer came and the heat was unbearable, they had decamped to the college's summer villa, in the Alban Hills a few hours out from the city. The Palazzola, as it was called, was perched on a hill overlooking a lake, and they all had hill- or lake-view rooms. There was a pool there too, and on summer evenings after catechetics classes, they'd been known to run into it naked, sometimes joined by a tutor or two, and an older member of the college would creak open a shutter above and call good-naturedly to them to ask that they keep it down. They'd snatch Chianti in big basket jugs from the pantry, and drink it from the bad glasses, while overhead the Perseids or the Lyrids or the Arietids – or whichever ids were streaking through the skies – strummed their silent songs against the dome. David had loved it all, the lean tanned forearms and the shoe salesmen standing in the doors of their shops smoking as though they were lords of great domains, the feline way the young men moved when they fought in the streets on a Saturday night. He loved to see his contemporaries, the English men of the English College, learning about steamed milk and soft cheeses and bitter leaves dressed in olive oil. He watched them all exhale slowly into the sensualism of this place. There had been a gorgeous, mellifluous camaraderie to it. They ran through the ruins at night and practised their projecting among the tombs of lesser emperors. They goaded one another to burst the burrata as it wobbled in the bowl, to roll the young red wine over their tongues, to suck the juice through a single bite of the peaches when they arrived, to slice the cured meat very thinly and eat it ruffled onto airy bread. These were not things which could be renounced. They were prerequisite, in Rome. The men who today moved their limbs through the waters of the pool would be returning to England, with its meteorological meekness, but they did so with the unshakeable knowledge of passeggiata and sprezzatura.

He loved the Latin of the Mass, or of his lessons – always had – the mouthfeel of the words; their weight as he shaped each one for the master. Its rigid demand and answer. When he'd arrived in Italy he'd had to get used to Italian's blowsiness, how the words ran into one another with such wanton ease. They were immediately sent to philosophy lessons in Italian at the Gregorian University, or Greg, as they called it, even though none of them could speak Italian. It was assumed that with their command of Latin they could just cotton on, and they sort of did. Lectures were five hours a day, five days a week, with no audience participation (so they said, ruefully, amongst themselves). They would stop for ice cream on the way home, eating sweet stracciatella with tiny spoons from paper cups.

He liked being told what to do. He liked waking up knowing what he had to wear in the morning. He liked the awareness of himself as a being in a hierarchy, with people above and below him. He liked all the secret codes and small rituals: shoe-polishing on Sundays, its rhythms learnt at eight years old in the long communal bedrooms of school, the sound of sixty sisal brushes whisking over sixty pairs of shoes; when and where to turn up and be fed. He liked his presence being demanded in a particular place at a particular time, and the fact that there would be consequences if you didn't appear. Knowledge of consequences was what propelled him through so many of the days.

Sundays were their busiest. They were encouraged to go to Mass in a different church each week and see whose style they liked best. They were sorted into teams of three, and had to go in the rig, and greet the priest afterwards. They forced themselves to speak in broken Italian although they all knew Latin would work too.

They were taught about wine.

The ads for cleaners read: 'Only plain girls need apply'.

Here by the pool, newly ordained and on the eve of their departure, they felt glamorous. David was caught off-guard by the pleasure of this sensation. He languished in it, until someone splashed water onto his chest, and he rose, strode to the end where the diving board was, walked, bounced once. Someone in the pool would have seen the clean shape of him rise, the arms coming together and the muscles of the legs pulling into sharper focus, pure form against the sun, and then slip into the water with a murmur to its surface, sending nets of light over the tiles beneath.

3

DAVID WAS TWENTY-NINE, older than the usual but not by much, and it was not so rare now; the war had bumped them up a couple of years, so that his intake had been a mix of eighteen-year-olds who'd been too young to enlist, and men in their mid-twenties and beyond, with tales of the Bulge or Dunkirk. He was too old to think in terms of destiny, but he was ready and eager for his coming work. Now, walking to meet his parents for dinner, he was wearing a suit and cufflinks which had been a twenty-fifth birthday present, originally an engagement present from his mother to his father. They hadn't celebrated his twenty-fifth because seminarians were only allowed to go home once over the course of their training. Tonight was only the second time he had seen his parents in seven years, and before that the intervals weren't all that much better. They hadn't celebrated his twenty-first either – he'd been deployed in Rangoon – and before the war there had been the navigation course in Québec City, and before that Oxford, and finally, to begin, school.

Oxford was the only place he'd been where there hadn't been a uniform. It had left him feeling slightly shapeless, like unproved dough. He was reading Maths, a decision for which he'd had to summon a stubbornness he did not possess. Father Stuart, at school, had leant across his desk and said, again, 'Classics would really be my first choice for you, my boy.' Classics was always first choice. But he liked maths; he liked balancing the scales of it to get at a double-sided truth. And it was classicism, of a kind, which ran back and back through wars and trades, and told the story of the Mediterranean, Carthage, Sparta, the prime of the Athenians.

He had only been at university for two of his three years when the war came knocking. It was 1944. He was twenty. He trained to be an aerial navigator on a base in Canada. That was where he'd met Marie, the one and only entry in the annals of his sexual experience. They'd mainly fumbled around in her car in the dark and the snow, too cold and too clothed to do much. It had lasted all of three weeks before he was shipped out, first to perform raids on German prisons, complicated operations involving bombing the sides of the buildings in order to breach them, thereby permitting the prisoners' escape. Then onwards, to Burma, where he was in charge of a POW camp – they were encouraged to use the word 'coolies' or 'Japs'. He was there until he was demobbed. Early on in his posting was a moment which became family legend. A British navy ship docked in Rangoon, and David was among those who received it. The onboard naval navigator was none other than Ralph, eighteen and on his first job. 'That's my brother!' they had yelled rawly at one other across the gangplank.

He went on a single tour of the city's brothels, on the insistence of some of the other men in his unit. The alleyways they were found down, with their jaundiced light, and fellow British soldiers pissing up against their walls, their little mounds of vomit slicking the stones, filled him with a sour sadness. He felt nothing for the girls with their slack hair, in the dirty rooms which low lamps did little to disguise. All told, that was that.

Then the Americans dropped the bombs on those unsuspecting cities whose names would now be for ever twinned. The reports began to trickle back. There had been a great white flash, sliding through the sky like a dropped knife, and people woke up clutching their own tripe in their hands. He knew what it meant, and the war's end washed over him. He lay in his quarters with his face to the wall. He felt he needed to make a grand gesture of his life to atone. There was a blood debt which must be paid. He hated his and his troops' proximity to it, as if he could smell the great acridity of American sin floating over west on the wind. He dreamt of the burnt, the skin of whose wrists and hands, it was said, had come off like opera gloves when they reached out to be helped into boats.

The next morning, someone passed an English-language newspaper through the fence into one of the prisoners' pens. The British stood by in clusters, watching and smoking. The more senior officers made the odd comment about it being ungentlemanly, an upstart move from a juvenile nation. One or two, who claimed more experience with the Far East, said this was the only way to deal with the Japs. Like an ant farm, said one. Strike the colony and they all rush back. David wiped his hand over his brow and watched the prisoners squatting on the other side of the wire, the paper increasingly shaking in their hands.

One or two Japanese officers spoke English, and they read the paper hurriedly. A murmur of panic began to move through the enclosures. Men in other pens walked up to the fences, putting their hands round bald sections of barbed wire, and began calling questions to each other. Then the rains came. The prisoners tried to keep reading, but the newspaper was shaken from their hands into a pulp. Those who had read the words in English began shouting the news in Japanese. Within ten minutes all the men had been informed, and some were keening on the duckboards, covering their faces with filthy shirts and revealing the runnels of dirt on their bodies beneath.

Then the eerie thing: they stopped. They sat down, cross-legged and straight-backed, and were completely quiet. And it was like that, by and large, until they were gone.

The emperor made the announcement of Japan's capitulation, and then the British had to send their prisoners home. They opened the pens with bolt-cutters, great sections of wire springing slack. The Japanese stood up with a flinty composure, and filed out neatly. The British loaded them onto ships.

He was discharged in 1946. Upon returning home to England, he had gone immediately to his archbishop and declared his intentions.

At the restaurant, his mother had changed from her church black into a purple dress and matching bolero jacket of shot silk, which shone crimson in the candlelight. She wore her pearls. She stood to greet him. His father shook his hand. They settled back into the booth. It was dark and women smoked, wearing gloves. His parents held hands above the bright, clean tablecloth and toasted him. They ordered spaghetti to start, and David had to teach them how to eat it. Claire laughed gamely as it splashed, threatening to stain Edwin's shirt. Then pork with white beans and stalks of celery, and panna cotta to finish.

They found an enoteca and had a nightcap, but Claire and Edwin declared the place 'too young' for them. He supposed what they meant was that they'd had their fill of foreignness for the day, so he walked his parents back to their hotel. They had a week's driving holiday through Tuscany booked, and would meet him once they were all back in England.

It was only ten or thereabouts, and his dress shoes were well worn in and gritted against the cobbles, so he kept walking, at first with no destination in mind, and then ended up on the Appian Way in the dark, where he sat on some long-fallen pediment for a few hours, kicking the dust, watching the sky and discerning its shapes. Then back via the Colosseum, the Forum, extending the route slightly to encompass the Pantheon. He was not alone. There were other young men dressed as he was (black trousers, black shirt, Roman collar) and solitary, his newly appointed colleagues, of a kind. The city was full of them. He walked slowly, swilling the still summer air. He remembered nights in Oxford, wearing this suit, filling it perfectly, stumbling up Queen Street singing, other boys' arms around and on either side of him, the vague pull of hoping for women to look at, to talk to shyly if they got drunk enough.

He arrived back at the English College as the night was

shading to grey. He sat in the chapel and looked at the paintings of the martyrs high on the walls in the growing light: poor Ralph Sherwin who hadn't lasted very long, four months of 1543, before he was found and met a brutal end, the pistons of his limbs popped from their joints and pulled; the hanging, the drawing, the quartering. And all those who came after, whose demises were painted gorily on the walls in an attempt at Delft blue.

When the first bells began to ring, he went upstairs to his room. He undressed and sat to polish his shoes, then changed into his cassock. No one was awake to see him slip away. The dawn was slow and sloe-coloured.

At the station cafe, he sat down outside and ordered a cappuccino. He put on his sunglasses and smoked a cigarette.

All about him were signs of the city's rousing. Young children with school satchels bouncing on their backs. Women walking dogs, already impeccably dressed and wearing low brogued heels, and hats. Old men buying newspapers from young men on bicycles. People pushing flower carts, water lilting out of buckets filled with apricot-coloured roses.

His train will be for Milan initially, then Paris. From there: Calais. The ferry to Dover. A train to London, and onwards to Birmingham. He is very lucky to be posted to his home archdiocese.

He dropped change loudly in the saucer. He had always liked the china they used in cafes here: thick, like sinks. He liked its acoustic quality when the sheet-stamped steel spoon hit it.

He practised flattening the vowels just right. Where to make the sounds in his mouth. The burr to roll under his Rs.

Out of the train window there would be the meek countryside, the high summer of lone oaks in the middles of fields. The soft bodies of English hills. He hadn't seen them in years, and now he would be home, for ever.

    He had been called, he felt it ring within him like a bell. He would minister to the sick and dying, he would splash babies' heads, and those of men and women who wished to join the fold for love, like his father had; he would anoint young men and women into the vocations of family and fruitfulness. He would dispense the word of the Lord to that wayward island. He would pass through the Flaminian gate and back to that godless island flung off the northernmost edge of the continent, where the old faith clung on in pockets, where his work was to make it bloom again. He would be at the coalface of life, performing the rituals associated with its stages, and yet he would be somewhat apart from it. This suited him, so he told himself.

4

2018

ADRIAN CALLED HIS mother again the day after the funeral, on the walk to Tottenham Hale and the Stansted Express, his flight to Nîmes. It was before dawn in London, a winelight Sunday evening in Berkeley. This time she picked up – Darling! He fumbled for the rage of the day before, the sense of betrayal, of having been under-briefed, and, looming large behind the immediate social embarrassment: the vast unknowing which had meant he hadn't known the word, *laicization*, hadn't known how to spell it, had got it wrong and then been steered by the suggested alternative search result.

– Darling! Calm down. You're right. I'm sorry. I didn't know either. Not till he was really ill. She was eating almonds. He could hear them giving way under her teeth. – There was a knock at the door one day, when I was there helping to look after him, and there was this man on the doorstep saying he was the Archbishop of Birmingham. Ralph was there too, he'd brought him. They asked to see Gung, and so I took them both up there and left them to it, I had some cooking to do. Then I was summoned.

Adrian's anger subsided slightly. He could sense that this secret, which was not, in his mother's case, a secret per se, more a thing willfully forgotten, had been tightly wound for a very long time, and now she was throwing it across to him, hard, and it was unspooling rapidly in the air between them.

– My father in those days was on a lot of morphine. But he asked me to go get my mother and then when we were all there he held our hands and said, Hilary, there is something you must know. And then he told me: Before I met your mother, I was a Catholic priest. Just like that. And that, now that he was dying, he wanted to be made lay again – as in, become a layperson again. That's why the archbishop had come. To meet him and hear his case, because pleas like that have to go all the way up through the canon lawyers at the Vatican, something like that, and you need the archbishop of the place where you were a priest before to help, to vouch for you, so you can be officially released from your vows and forgiven for trespassing against them or some crap. It was all so upsetting and confusing, and you were so little then anyway. I went for a long walk and cried for hours.

She will be wanting to have a bath before she goes to bed. He feels he can sense her glancing towards the bathroom door in anticipation. He knows that she has just begun the school year by teaching *Dracula* to her high school students, and she is enjoying it.

– He said the whole thing could take months, and he held out for it, he really did. And I couldn't understand why a forgiving god would need something so . . . bureaucratic. It made me think heaven, or the waiting room to heaven or whatever, was like the queue for immigration at the airport, and this was just some sort of entry visa. It felt *medieval*, and it made me so angry. Anyway it arrived, it was an actual piece of paper, and then three days later he died. I'm not joking.

Her voice had thickened now. He had reached the station. A light rain had started up and could be seen falling in the sodium orbs of the streetlights.

– Listen, sweetheart, I have to go.

In the end no one asked about the crucifix at Customs. The plane bore down towards the Alps and then banked west, coming in low over the pink squares of the salt farms and the sea, arriving on the runway bordered by olive trees, where the airport was a single room not much bigger than a barn. Adrian caught the bus and it drove windingly through the villages, their walled cemeteries cornered with gnarled cypress trees, their pétanque pitches and caves coopératives, the public potted oleanders. He'd been coming here all his life: it was where his grandmother had lived, for nearly forty years. This was where he'd learnt to swim and cook and kiss and ride a bike, and every time he returned to it he felt all the red rooms of his heart rejoice. In his London life, he spoke no French, and whenever he returned to France he spent about ten days rummaging in the bottom drawer of his mind for the grammar of it. He loved how the light went gold in the trees. He loved the hardy life, for all its tenacity also so graceful: the wild thyme, the olive trees with their knotted elbows, the vines' spread and spent shoulders on the wires, the heron who haunted one particular stretch of river and whom he saluted when he swam in the early mornings and evenings. The place names flicked past on their red-bordered white signs. He knew their order by heart.

He had come because his grandmother had had a fall. That dreaded formulation, and all the possibilities it dragged with it: 'had a fall' was euphemism for 'the beginning of the end'. It was the hopeful expression that the dying process had now begun, and wouldn't be too disgusting to behold. He had heard stories of his friends' grandparents, lying in their hallways for three days with broken hips and no one to find them, or falling down the stairs and – bang, they said. That was that. Or strokes which smote them and three days later: they'd be dead. Or lesser strokes, which left them watching *The Sound of Music* on loop for twelve years, while they lay in enormous padded armchairs. 'Had a fall' was a catch-all, it contained so many emotions and allowed you to articulate them publicly all at once. 'Had a fall' was the punctum, the turn twenty minutes before the end of the film, the warning shot. It began the priming process. 'Had another fall' was worse, because it was not the finite narrative trope that some secretly prayed it would be.

His grandmother had had another fall a week before Ralph's funeral. She had been walking in the village and claimed to have 'found herself falling'. She had fallen on her face. There had been blood, lots of it, which made it look worse than it was. Neighbours had picked her up and called an ambulance. They visited her in hospital and brought her clean clothes. Tests were run, but nothing noteworthy appeared on them. Her bones were unbroken. She was back home within a few days, but her confidence had been knocked, and she was afraid to leave the house.

The school where his mother worked would be reluctant to let her go for a crisis as open-ended as this. Whereas Adrian had finished university; he was applying for jobs; he needed a cheap place to live. So they decided that it would be him who went to his grandmother. He had stood in

London pubs and told his friends, with unconvinced gestures, of his plans, the conversations repeating. But won't you be lonely? Do you have friends there? That sounds like a lot.

When he arrived, his grandmother was asleep in her chair. He climbed the stairs to the guest room, what had been his grandfather's room, and hung the crucifix on the prominent hook that had been, he supposed, its sticking-place before. Its dark wood was the colour of a putrescence, and the small corpse like shrivelled lilies, curdled milk, lard. He shut the door on the guest room and left it stoppered there, climbing higher into the house to his habitual room. In the fridge: a single wizened carrot dangling between the wire struts of a shelf, two yogurts, a boiled beetroot on a saucer, half a cheese.

There was no car, so he woke early to get out the bicycle. He had pulled the blue frame from a skip as a teenager. He had attached a metal drawer from a freezer to the back rack of the bike with zip ties. Now he pumped both tyres and rinsed the rims with soapy water. The supermarket was a forty-minute ride away. He cycled by the back roads, past the fields and their alternating crops of wine and wheat and oil. The vines rowed on in their swift orthogonals. He bought only as much as he could carry, but still he needed bleach and a heavy box of Marseille soap. He filled his rucksack with a modest litany of things he thought she'd like: white fish and leeks; Jerusalem artichokes to roast; many kinds of grain and beans, the wherewithal for several soups; citrus fruit. The seasonal wind which rushed down the Rhone each winter buffeted him sidelong all the way home. A certain speed was necessary for the balance of his load. If he stood up out of the seat, he felt his centre of gravity shift; he thought of the eggs wobbling in the dark of their carton. The sun was warm on the back of his neck. The river gorge ran along on the right.

5

SHE HAD MADE no plans to live so long.

She had made no plans to live so long, and therefore Adrian and Hilary had to make the arrangements, and this engendered rage on every side.

They decided that she needed to be moved to the ground floor. Adrian converted the dining room into her new bedroom, padding it with rugs and lamps, building bookshelves. She kept saying heavily, 'I don't know about this,' standing in the way, sighing. Always when she spoke like this, Adrian was crouching somewhere beneath her, on the ground with a drill, putting up brackets, reassembling furniture.

He swam in the river every day. Sometimes in the morning, waking at sunrise to walk out of the village, past the allotments and the cherry orchards, with a thermos of coffee and a croissant scrunched in a paper bag. There would be long fish leaping vertically out of the water to catch insects in the middle distance. Once, he saw the azure flinch of a kingfisher against the opposite bank. Other days, he would wait until the evening, after he had made them both dinner and was clearing their plates, and tell her he needed to go, he wanted

to swim. Yes, yes, she would say, with a queenly wave of her hand, and one evening:
– He liked to do that too.

It was the first time in his life that he looked at her properly. What he saw was a very old woman in need of a haircut. Her silver hair stood out in bars around her cheeks. The lower lids of her eyes: loosened, and seeping. Her hands gnarled like mooring rope.

When she'd hit her late eighties, she'd begun to decline in strange, unpredictable zigzags. She left the stove on, the tap running, the front door on the latch when she went to the bakery, or ground-floor windows wide open. When he and his mother visited, they found ziplock bags full of soil in the tea caddy, or what must have been plums once, judging by their stones, moulding in lidded casserole dishes on the counter.

Her grasp on time fascinated him. When she said 'some years ago' she could be talking about the 1970s, and 'the other day' took on its literal and indifferent sense of 'any day which is not this day'. She was the last left standing of her friends, the woman who walked by herself through the years: all the days of the present were alike to her. Women in their forties were 'young girls'. She would launch into sentences with great intakes of breath, and then stop and stall on missing words. He watched her panicked fumble for *chest of drawers*, *handbag* and *shower*. She gestured in frustration at a chunk of history which had blurred. 'You know,' she said, 'that German monk who made all the fuss.' She meant Martin Luther.

Time slowed, became brackish. He moved his body

through the labours of the day. He kept the hours of her needs and meals. At night sleep was like a force upon his limbs.

When she made shopping lists for him, she gave lengthy justifications for the purchase of yogurt or cologne, her reasoning like a network of calcified pipes that water must push through. He learnt to anticipate what she would find difficult: unfamiliar voices on the phone. Fastening her seatbelt. Opening a teabag. Operating the pill organizer.

His mother had applied to the département to have his grandmother added to a waiting list for a care home, but they hadn't told her yet. They agreed that it was best to wait until a spot became available, and present her with the fait accompli.

Soon it was October. The vines had turned red and dropped their leaves, and the cuttings burnt on bonfires which scented the late afternoons. His nana was cold, constantly. He called the village's one-man forestry service and ordered firewood, then spent hours stacking it by the back door.

She spent most of her days on the sofa. She would get dressed, always in elaborate outfits: a coordinated jumper or cardigan, a small silk scarf knotted and fastened at her throat with a brooch. Shoes.

She had a new pain in her neck and she needed another X-ray to check it. He had to undress her at the clinic. It was the first time he had ever seen her naked. He had never even seen her shoulders before and now he crouched at her feet carefully rolling her stockings back from her shins. She was afraid, he could see, and so he stood up and stroked her hair.

Another thing he'd never done before. She leant back into his touch and breathed deeply with her eyes closed.

Sometimes stupendous clarity would come upon her in flashes. They were discussing the 2002 Boston clerical abuse scandal because they had just watched the film *Spotlight* together, and he had used the word paedophilia.
– It's not paedophilia, she said. *Paedophilia* means love of children. It is not love of children. It is child abuse.
There were touring Jehovah's witnesses stationed in Nîmes, who, having surmised that an old lady lived alone in the house, knocked on the door. She kept them standing on the doorstep for over half an hour, throwing questions at them like javelins.

In the evenings, he called his mother. She would be on her lunch hour, eating salad from a box.
– I just remember, when Daddy was dying, Cousin James saying, 'There's a story they'll be taking to their graves,' she said.
– But what was it? An affair?
– I don't *know*, darling.
He understands he is asking his mother to retread ground she has long since chosen to leave behind. In her background: playground sounds.
– When I asked them about it, they said it was an intellectual decision. Something about their ideas no longer being tenable within the institution of the Church. There was a bitten pause. She was folding a lettuce leaf with her fork. – But then there was James, alluding to this great love story. It

only occurred to me much later that it could be both, I suppose.

– And you never spoke to them about it again?

– No. After he died, I felt cheated by the whole thing. I didn't want to know. I had my life over here, in Berkeley, and I had you, and that's what I wanted. I suppose I also had a certain deference. He had obviously wanted to take the finer points of it all to his grave.

– But what about her?

– What do you mean?

– You never spoke about it with her?

– No.

There were things in his mother's relationship with her own mother which his mother spoke about and others which she didn't. He let it be.

He resolved to try to get his grandmother talking on the subject.

They were sitting on the sofa. He was sewing her name into her socks, in preparation for the day she would be moved out of the house.

– Nana.

– Yes.

– You and Gung.

She made a wary noise in her throat. Her noise for not suffering fools gladly.

He decided to be as clear and blunt as possible.

– When he was still a priest. Did you have an affair?

She straightened her back and folded her hands into the curve between her thighbones, near the knees.

– Oh. That whole business.

She levelled an igneous look at him. Her eyes gathered their colour, like a storm massing on the line of the sea.

– You mean did we make love before he was defrocked?

She was like this. If you found the right question, she would meet you at it, a reward for having found a suitable angle of approach.

– Yes.

– You are missing the point. About celibacy. It is about so much more than sex.

She was like this too. Elusive. Flashing through the deep and the dark, like a fish.

– But sex is about so much more than sex, Nana. It's about the body, and life in the here and now.

He tested a turn of phrase he thought would appeal to her: – It's about seizing the fleeting.

– Mmm. Point taken.

Then she struggled to her feet and across the room, using the precise placement of the furniture as a sequence of holds. He heard her shuffling in the kitchen with the kettle.

6

1956

THERE WERE THINGS about Rome David missed. The theatre of its streets. How speech came so easily and volubly between strangers. Strolling the village green in his Roman collar, he still turned heads, but there now was an element of reverence to it. His own singularity was new: he was the lone priest posted here; there was no one to walk beside him and share in the heat of the villagers' gaze.

The place was Monks Kirby, a prim commuting village in the orbit of Birmingham, with a clipped green and a standard-issue war memorial. The congregation was composed of the Old Catholic families, who claimed their lineage from the Recusants who'd held firm, and had lived in the area for generations, their clothes expensive and brushed; and then there were some Irish, whose fathers had come over a few generations before and whose labour had built the canals of Birmingham, and the railways which linked it south. There were one or two Polish air force families, come over after the war, and with the fathers of these David was on emphatic, hand-shaking terms.

The congregation seemed ready for him and in those first years he slotted in and busied himself with conveying the authority they conferred upon him. His youth excited them. The outgoing priest, a Father Connolly, had been older, from County Mayo, and the English parishioners had curled their lips at him. When word spread that the new man was of good Staffordshire stock, back and back through generations, they'd been delighted. Finally someone in the head office had skimmed off the crème de la crème and sent it to them. From Rome, no less. Such was the talk in the queue at the butcher's.

His mother was a regular at his services. At first she came with his father, then alone. She sat straight-backed at the front, and always, afterwards, clasped his hand very hard and told him he was a natural, *so* charismatic, darling, I could watch you for *hours*.

On Thursdays he drove to the local hospital, to perform last rites and give the ill communion. Of all his duties this was his favourite. He enjoyed packing the bag with stole, Bible, chalice and host, the small bottle of wine, pulling up at the hospital car park and leaning out of the window to be enthusiastically waved through by the attendant. He loved the hush which quelled the lift when he entered it, the sentences which broke off or the sotto voce greetings, made in a reverent haste as they ascended, in their clean new box of glass and steel, towards the fourth floor, where he began.

For some time now his first patient had been twenty-two-year-old Sylvia Wilmer, who was dying of leukaemia. She was the reason he could never be late: they timed her morphine doses so that she would be lucid enough to receive communion. She had a drawn, angular face, and was a sallow colour, with bruise-like contouring of the jaw and brow. Her dark hair was cut short and hung limp and plain. She reminded him of a figure from some altar piece of the thirteenth century painted on wood, whose flesh tones had been underpainted with green earth and egg to bind properly to the panel of beech or ash or oak. How this green earth, over the years, began to corrode the peachy colours of the skin above it and show through, giving its subjects a gangrenous hue, an expression of the admonition that all flesh is grass.

When he rounded the corner into Sylvia's ward, the heels of his shoes smacking the linoleum, a smile would break upon her face like winter sunlight. – Father Fletcher! she would exclaim, and shuffle herself, with a half-suppressed wince, into a somewhat upright and attentive position. – Miss Wilmer, he'd say, as he pulled up a chair. She always asked him to call her Sylvia, saying each time that she thought her full name sounded so much better than Miss Wilmer.

– Sylvia Wilmer, she'd begin, with theatricality, the sentence hanging in the space of air between them, I want to hear as much as I can before I go. Then she asked about the weather and the driving conditions. – My father had been teaching me to drive, she'd say. She had wanted to be an actress or a poet, or both.

He came in spring – it was his third year in the parish, and tipping into his second of visiting Sylvia – and the window was open and through it they saw (and heard) the loud flapping of pigeons mating. She caught his eye straying over to the branch where it was happening, and she laughed at him. It was one of those days when he had arrived early and the morphine was still holding her webbed in its threads. She was convinced he was a sheep farmer and wanted to know how the lambing was going. She gave him advice on gardening. Then she touched his wrist to emphasize a point about how best to dig up dandelions on a lawn ('You have to use a fork, you see. A trowel just won't do, they have no root diversification, they just go straight down and if you slice it with a trowel they'll just come straight back up again'), one finger on the skin before his cuff began. He looked down at her hand and felt himself blush. His hand under hers seemed like something separate from them both, a slender translucent crustacean.

The next week she turned to him as he was preparing to leave and said: – Father Fletcher, don't bother to come next week. I shan't be here any more. He smiled with rushed benevolence and did not ask her what she meant. He did not really know how morphine worked and pictured it beading inside her like mercury, high in the quire of her blood, which was poisoning her anyway, and said no more. When the following week came, he set off with his usual confidence. The roads were clear and the day very fine, small strips of cloud high in the sky and the hedgerows pounding with hawthorn blossom. The hospital was its usual self, but as he came round the corner of the corridor, a nurse accosted him with a hand on his arm (he looked down at it, and had the funny shellfish feeling again). – She's gone, Father Fletcher, she said. All of twenty minutes ago.

Young Miss Wilmer had taken a deep breath and let it out slowly, and then no more. He looked over and saw that the thin bed lay plain and smoothed.

He descended to the morgue in the service lift. A place of thin cold light coming on bar by bar with vitreous sounds. The feet beneath the sheet were pale, so pale, and dappled from within, purple and green. He folded the sheet down past the face, the cloth heavy and starched like a catering napkin. The flesh had fallen back against the bones in the way that made all the faces of the dead sexless and strange. He tried to picture her as she could have been, years hence. She would have grown into those bones of the jaw and the brow. Her beauty would have been planed, coolly strong.

He exhaled slowly, then laid his hand over the forehead and made the familiar shapes of the words: *requiem aeternam, lux perpetua. Luceat ei.*

That Sunday, he spoke in church for the first time of the need to face death head-on.

– The Victorians, he began, were obsessed with death and in denial about sexuality.

Something, a breeze, a draft, a gathering gasp, moved through the pews.

– We, for our part (here he raised both hands to gather the congregation into his arms) have it somewhat the other way around, and to our great detriment: we are in denial about death. But we would do well to come to our deaths properly, to meet them nobly, with the best of our faculties. Here he made reference to the mass death of their recent, shared memory; he conceded that they might not want to think too much on it, but nevertheless, the people of God should not succumb to this existential prudishness.

There were weeks still where he revelled in the showmanship of it all, when he was aware of his beauty, his dash and wit, and what they were in service to. These weeks he was like the organ, a set of pipes played, he felt, from on high. And then there were the other weeks, like the week Sylvia died, where there was the tiniest gossamer hint of something he found himself unwilling to name. His purpose was to glide through the world and its pains. But Sylvia had gripped his wrist and stopped him short, and for a moment he'd been pulled from his groove. He was thirty-four and completely alone.

7

2018

It was a tense, busy Christmas of many errands. Hilary came to France, and together she and Adrian both visited a funeral parlour to choose a plan, a prerequisite of entry to a care home. The woman they met with was kind, generous with her time. She made them coffee and listened to more of their story than was necessary. She had a frankness about her, which he found compelling. It was the same with all the other women (and it was, overwhelmingly, women) whom they met in this line of work and those related to it: the nurses and the carers in the multiple retirement homes they had been to visit. These women were in middle age; they gave them an hour or more of their time and patiently answered all their questions. They swung great bunches of keys on the ends of lanyards. They modulated their speech when they came across a resident in the halls. They wore their hair in simple twists with big clips and swung their hips. They were compassionate, and gentle, but also blunt, about the body and its loosening hold on its various functions. He found this quality somehow incredibly sexy, and it soothed him.

The two of them ran around compiling the long list of documents needed for the dossier to send to social services when the time came: marriage certificates and birth certificates spanning a generation in both directions, tax returns. It was while they were looking for these that they found something they didn't know what to make of.

A box file fell open in Adrian's hands and yielded a miscellaneous sheaf of papers. One was an anthology of feminist rewritings of hymns dating from the 1980s. Its pages carried the ghost of a dog-ear, and an underlining: 'I am Jezebel of ill-renown / who met death wearing her crown'. There was a typewritten article with his grandmother's name on it, a confusing extended metaphor about pigeons and the female pronouns used for the Holy Spirit in the Old Hebrew Bible. Beneath the article, the author bio read: 'Margaret Bendelow studied divinity at Regina Mundi in Rome.'

– Did you know about this? Adrian moved the article into his mother's line of sight. She was running something through the scanner.

Hilary's eyes slid over it. Her hand stilled on the feeder tray.
– What?

Adrian heard, in the word, the wind being knocked out of her. He went to make them tea.

When he came back, Hilary was sitting curled forward on the sofa with the heel of her hand pressed between her eyes.

– I don't have time for this! She squeezed a tear from each lower lid and dabbed at her nose.

– What does it mean, do you think?

– I have no idea. I just can't deal with this right now.

They put the box file back. He would return to it later, on his own.

✤

When, in January, after Hilary had gone home to California, a place became available in a home in the nearby market town, it felt as if it might be too soon. But the district nurse assured him: it is a miracle that it is so nearby, and best to do it *quand elle a toujours sa tête*. He would have to break it to his grandmother by himself. – I'm so sorry, sweetheart, said his mother over the phone, but he was happy to do this for them both, because he knew that he still had it in him to do it gently.

He knelt by the arm of his grandmother's chair. He held her hands and squeezed them. – Nana, I am sorry that it has come to this. I love you, he said, and I am going to look after you. Do not worry.

They sat looking at one another for a long time, him smoothing his thumb over her knuckle all the while. She was, he could see, furious. He could think of nothing more to say. Eventually he made to leave the room and start cooking. – Is this really necessary? she said as he turned to open the door. Her voice like rock. Her gaze of gunmetal. He could only think to nod, once, and then left the room quickly.

The next day, he sat in the chair opposite hers sewing more name tags into her clothes and linens. She stayed silent for two hours, and then, when he was getting up to cook again, she said – Why are you doing this to me? He had to launch into the explanation again. He knelt, he squeezed her hand. This time it was harder.

It was the same again the next day.

Then his mother came back again, using up her sick days to do so. They ordered two hundred more name tags and together sewed them into all of his grandmother's clothes and towels. They split the skin on their fingertips with the effort. They made cushion covers and went back and forth in the car with furniture. They took her orchids, her toiletries, a small selection of mugs. The room in the home, they agreed, was beautiful. It had a balcony overlooking the river. It got the morning sun.

The night before they moved her, he and his mother got drunk. They walked to the river and drank a whole bottle of wine, then came home and did the same again over dinner. It was then that Hilary spoke more about her father's death. They sat on the sofa, remnants of a risotto crusting in the kitchen.

– There was one afternoon, where he wanted to recite the *Dream of Gerontius* in the original but couldn't remember it, and he started crying about having lost his Latin, so Nana said it for both of them. He put his head in her lap and she ran her fingers through his hair. It was beautiful, Hilary was saying, and I never got a beautiful moment like that with him.

The phrase Hilary always used about her father's death was 'turned his face to the wall'. Her head was now in Adrian's lap, and she had started to cry.

– Do you know why he became a priest?

– No. She paused. He played with a strand of her hair. – I've never been able to crack it for myself. My father was a man inclined to such . . . silliness. And sensuality. He loved it when my mother got dressed up, put on her heels and jewellery, and perfume. He was a man who loved parties and pre-prandial drinks and dancing; he loved good food and skinny-dipping. When the first asparagus came into season he always exclaimed over it and dressed it in perfect mousseline sauce. He taught me to make orecchiette by hand, hold my drink, grill a fish wrapped in a fig leaf, basic carpentry. Quite a biblical skillset, in hindsight.

A dry laugh rises in her. Then she is quiet, and the mood drops like pressure. He can see it in the angle of her chin. – Once, though, she begins, I did ask him about the war. We were playing chess, late at night. I must have been fifteen or so. And he said something. But then he saw immediately he'd said too much, so he just shut down and we never spoke about it again.

– What did he say? He watches his mother reach for it in the back room of her memory.

– He said . . . She takes a deep breath and sits up to take a long slow sip of her tea. – Something about the prisoner of war camp.

This much they both knew.

– He said . . . someone died. Someone was killed. She was tapping the tips of her fingers against her mug. – There was a murder. And him in charge of clean-up.

       Chunks.   Spread all over.   With a machete.

The next day, the day of Margaret's departure, there was a boar cull underway. Hunters with hi-vis and long sideburns stood spaced along the road, their Jeeps parked at steep angles on the verges of the vineyards, their rifles pointing skyward. Adrian helped his nana with her coat, into the car, away from her house, and over the hills.

She would be there for three years.

8

1958

DAVID PERFORMED HIS brother's marriage ceremony. He had done a few weddings by then, but nevertheless he was nervous. And hungover. The night before he and Ralph had peeled off after dinner with their parents and gone to a pub. Then back to the house for whiskey stolen from their father's study, and then for a walk at dawn in rumpled clothes.

– You know it's my job to ask you if you're sure. David had his hands in his pockets as he walked. He could see Ralph eyeing the brambles on either side of the lane, their fruits still clenched red and green. Their entire childhood, before time became a thing cut up into terms and half-terms, could be mapped onto this one lane descending from their parents' house to this thin river.

– No, that's the best man's! And you're not. The ferrous smell of the water rose up to meet them on scraps of mist. Behind the line of hills, the sky was blanching a pale blue.

– You know what I mean.

– Yes, I'm sure.

Anna was a young woman from the village they'd met at the fête the previous summer. She'd been standing on the opposite edge of the common in a dress of signal green. Ralph had strode over to her with, as his friends teased him later, cucumber levels of cool. Her hair was fastened low at her neck with a black Bakelite hairslide. She turned to him like a planet on its axis, and he was confronted with her full attention. There were freckles on the bones of her cheeks.

Then they did all the usual things, Ralph told him. Trying to get the measure of what life with one another might look like. He let slip, over pints, that he loved her elbows more than anything he'd ever seen (David frowned good-naturedly into the foam of his beer). They went boating, Ralph told him, and lay in the grass, alone, eating bread and cheese with green-tomato chutney her mother made. She came to watch him play cricket. They went to dances and when he got to put his hands on her waist for the first time he thrummed like the flame of a stove. So he asked her, and she said yes.

Ralph spread his hands over the table of the pub. His look said this was a thing over which he had no power. – All joys are made generous and grand in her presence, he said. David threw his head back and laughed. This was his own idiom, which Ralph always teased him of taking beyond the pulpit. To encounter it in his brother's mouth gave him a feeling of some membrane silvering between them, some slippage.

Now, on the morning of the wedding, the brothers ambled down to the river and stripped off for a swim, roaring with the cold nude sluice of it. Then back to their childhood room, which they'd shared, to sleep until being woken a couple of hours later by their mother, who was frenzied and already wearing her suit. Ralph and David exchanged a grin. David went downstairs to where his new vestments hung in the hall cupboard and changed in the downstairs bathroom. He had been all the way to Liverpool to choose them, and had settled on a palette of cream and turquoise, with embroidered silvered stags leaping on its bib. He knew it would match his mother's clothes and she would be delighted with this fact. Sure enough, when he came out of the bathroom, she let out a yelp of delight. They took family photos in the living room.

It was the pride of his life to do this for his brother, he thought. He drove them both to the church and they sat there before the Kodak-snapping crowds came in, Ralph slouching on a pew in his rented morning coat.

– I will ask again.
– Dave!
– Just one more time.
– Don't be ridiculous!
– To be sure.
– Yes. Yes, I'm sure.
– There's a side door. Just give me the signal and I can get you out.

Looking at his brother, he was met with the fact that Ralph had creases at the corners of his eyes exactly like his own, and the same nose. And his brother was about to move into a place of which he, David, knew so little, though he advised people on their marriages all the time, when they came with dispatches from that often-troubled place. He ran the marriage classes for engaged couples: they had to log twenty hours of lessons with him before they could be married in church. Ralph had laughed when he'd offered for him and Anna join his next course. His thinking had been to spare them the fire and brimstone approach, what they secretly called the rosary rattler method, of Ralph and Anna's own parish priest, who was considerably older. But they had opted for him in the end, and Ralph reported back that he'd told them, and the assembled company, that they shouldn't be too alarmed if the occasional plate flew in their lives together. David had raised an eyebrow at this, but made a note of it nonetheless. It certainly sounded like a wise, worldly thing to say, and perhaps, when he himself was older and more experienced, he would feel able to say it.

The church was filling now. David winked at Ralph, who winked back. They assumed their places. It occurred to David, not for the first time, that this ceremony was an age-old staging and approving of sex, and he one of its main players. This is what David thought as the men and women filed in, in hats and suits. The doors opened and in came Anna, wearing white, flowers in her hair and hands, the nails in the heels of her white satin-covered shoes clipping the sliced stone of the floor.

The homily was well received. At the reception afterwards, David earned cheers with his dancing. A small girl tried to teach him the jive and he gamely emulated her, to much applause. These were people he'd known his whole life, mostly related to him. He felt silly and joyous and important. And free. Anna took her veil off and they danced a waltz. Then he waltzed with his mother, who was balmily drunk, such that she kept rubbing her cheeks, complaining that they hurt too much from all the smiling.

A year later, when he held the first of the people that his brother and Anna made, with its randomly waving legs, his pride at his younger brother doubled over on itself. He looked from Ralph to the baby with eyes that welled. – Well

done, he said, then put the baby down and clapped him on the back. Ralph couldn't seem to take his eyes off his wife or child, and was always touching one or the other.
— What was it like?
— What was what like?
— You know.
— The birth?
— Mm-hmm.
— Well, when I came in after it was all over I thought at first I'd never seen Anna so angry. She was so red in the face.
The babies came thick and fast after that: it was one every two years for his whole first decade in Monks Kirby. Ralph and Anna's money stretched. They couldn't afford fresh fruit and David always tried to bring some whenever he came, which was almost every other weekend. They bought an old ambulance, gutted it, and fitted it with benches for the family transport. Anna was always knitting, it seemed to him. She could sit for hours, only her hands moving, the needles ticking against one another like some primordial clock that held the whole house together. She used it for prayer, she told him. It was such a gift, she said, her stomach swelling week by week as she said it, and I have so many cardigans to make. When the older ones began walking it was a wonder to David, their stocky, strangely jointed bodies venturing forth with a blunt and greedy curiosity. How, when he picked one up, it would root for his hip and latch on there. Once at Sunday lunch she was weightily pregnant and wearing a thin sundress, and a small pod-shaped surface protruded slightly, passing the circumference of the dome from within as if on a rail. He must have stared because she laughed at him. — It was just a hand! She was waving at you.

– How do you know it wasn't a foot?

– Because it didn't feel like a foot. Would you like to feel it?

He would. He got up and moved across the room to her and stood awkwardly at the arm of the chair. She smiled at him. He saw the truth then, in what was said about the beauty of pregnant women. Anna was not glowing, there was a small sheen of sweat on her nose, but she seemed wise, like a kind of mariner. She took his hand. He let her. She placed it on the pantheon of her belly. There was nothing at first, and for a moment the thought rose within him that he couldn't think if he had ever touched this part of a woman before, since he had become a man. But then something stirred, down there in the amber-dark. Something small and flat rose to meet him. He pictured the creature inside her, pressing its hand up against the cave wall, finding it pliant, finding something shifting from deep within the dome where it swam and floated out the days.

The older ones loved him and clamoured round his legs with their arms in the air when he came through the garden gate, as if receiving a great presence from above, which he supposed to them he was. If he could manage it, he scooped two of them up, one under each arm, and the others would run about underfoot, protesting for their turn. He taught some of the first ones to ride a bike, running back and forth up and down their cul de sac with one hand on the back of the same minute red bicycle and then letting go, hearing their shrieks of indignation, betrayal, and then eventual self-belief, glee. He bandaged miniature knees and hands and intoned 'the magic words', a protracted prayer, moving his fingers in front of their faces in the sign of the cross. After meals when he and Ralph sat in the living room, children would climb into their laps, back into them with wriggles. They would look at each other, both of them jigging the children on one knee, and laugh. He had never seen his brother so happy. David watched Ralph picking up the children that launched themselves at his legs, how they put their arms around his neck and nestled their tiny heads there. He watched how Ralph would place his hand on Anna's shoulder as she stood at the sink, or the small of her back as she deposited a dish at the centre of the table. He watched how Anna did the same, sometimes putting her hand on the back of her seated husband's neck, the casual way she ran her fingers through his hair.

He watched.

9

2019

She hated it, of course. When Adrian went to visit her in those first weeks, she would beg to be taken back home. She complained the other residents were weird. She didn't learn anyone's names. She said the food was awful. She said she had no access to the outdoors.

It took him an hour to cycle there.

At the beginning he went every other day; now he goes once a week, on a Wednesday.

Wednesdays are market days. He buys tapenade, sheep's cheese, pickled garlic and whatever produce is in season. He likes gaining an appreciation for each new offering: turnips, asparagus; later, wild strawberries, tiny perfumed apricots with deep daubs of crimson blush on their skins. He tries to bring his grandmother a small pleasure every time he visits, something he knows she will enjoy eating. He brings her every variety of olive: Lucques, first of the harvest, simply brined, crunchy, and still a blithe green; the black Grecques, wrinkled like palms; the buttery tender-fleshed Picholines, the small Cailletiers and their nuttiness, the colour of a city sky at night. He sits in the dining room of the second floor, where her room is, paring their flesh off with a butter knife. His grandmother feels for them on the plate, not looking, and eats them faster than he can de-stone them.

They both know that they are waiting for her to die.

He knows that looking after her is a form of care less well regarded, because it is ostensibly unproductive. It is a thing – a monumental feat of love composed of a thousand gritty, grubby, bone-wearying acts – which many people do not want to think about too clearly. When people express surprise at his caring for his grandmother, and tell him, wanting to comfort, that this is not his role, he starts to wonder if it is all an elaborate cover-up: the young are meant to be kept apart from the elderly because the world needs them to head into child-rearing blind, not to know how gruelling care for another is. Then again, he thinks, when he goes to bed every night, the exhaustion has a fulsome quality. He believes that what he is doing is worthwhile. Yes, he will place his hearing, the muscles of his legs and arms, at his grandmother's disposal; she will live with dignity and he will do this for her. For her, and for his mother.

He cycles back and forth between the village and the town. His trousers start falling lower round his hips. His obliques, or are they just his ribs, begin to show.

He cycles home and cries into the headwind: Please, let it be soon. Let it be swift, and painless, but please go.

At night, he scrolls through his friends' Instagram feeds, or watches TV on his laptop with the lights off, the screen splashing its aquarium colours on the ceiling. He tutors online; the money tides him over.

❖

His mother comes on her winter break, driving from Marseille in a rented car. She pings the scrunched drawstring of his pyjamas. – What's this, baby? she says. We don't like this. Sort it out. On his blue bicycle, the basket full of dishwasher salts and chickpeas on the way back from the supermarket, a lettuce wafting at the top of his open rucksack, he feels tough; he feels himself to be becoming one of the men he'd always aspired to be.

One morning, he is in line at the baker, and a middle-aged woman taps him on the shoulder. – *Vous êtes le petit fils de Madame Fletcher, n'est-ce pas?* Her hair is grey and pulled back from her face. She is wearing a shirt in a Provençal pattern, shades of blossom and rust. – *Oui*, he says.

– *Je suis Dominique, l'infirmière.* She has a deep tan. Her décolleté is freckled and bears deep lines. Past her uppermost button peeks the fig-coloured lace of her bra. She is asking him about his *mamie* and his *maman*. He explains his situation. He has reached the head of the queue, asks for two baguettes *tradition* and drops his change in the dish. She interrupts her talk to do the same. They wish the baker a *bonne journée*, her adding the regional half-syllable to *bonne*. She remembers, she says, his *grand-père*. He had been a *grand homme*, she says. They leave the baker, with their armfuls, and appear to be walking back towards the centre of the village together. The mistral has been blowing for three days.

– *C'était moi*, she says, *qui est venue lui donner les piqures.* Adrian's attention stumbles as he feels for the meaning of the last word. Pricking, stinging. Injections. *La morphine*, offers Dominique, searching his face. *Enfin, j'étais l'une des infirmières*. One of the nurses. Adrian remembers now that his mother had told him about the district nurses when his grandfather was dying, how they all commented on the fact that his pain threshold was abnormally high. It's dangerous, they'd told her. We don't know how much relief to give him.

He realizes that he has stopped and is looking at her blankly. He asks her if she would like to come back to the house for a coffee. – *Avec plaisir, jeune homme!* Her smile is a thing of generous beauty.

She says she remembers the kitchen table. She runs her hands along its edge. She tells him that she has sat and spoken with his mother at this table, and that his French is better now than his mother's had been then. Dominique had tried to reassure Hilary – pronounced, *Ilary* – about the impending death of her father, but *c'est tellement difficile*, in cases like that, *quand c'est si vite*. Fast. That's what they all said about his grandfather's death. He'd been given a year and he was dead in three months.

Dominique blows on her coffee and looks about the room. Did he know, she begins, that there was a *dame anglaise* in the next village over, part of her rounds, who several years prior, his *mamie* had helped while she was dying? He did not. He asks what her name was. Dominique says only it was *quelquechose très anglais, très romantique*, then snaps her fingers together: – Rosaline? Rosamund? Adrian shrugs. Dominique dives on, in the swim of it. This woman, Rosaline-Rosamund, had cancer. She was young, in her mid-fifties, and it was terminal. His grandmother had gone over to this woman's house, Dominique tells him, every day as far as she could tell, because she was always there when Dominique herself arrived, and the other nurses said the same of their rota days. His grandmother always offered her tea, she remembers – *Tellement anglais! C'etait très charmant.*

Did she know what his grandmother did with this woman? Adrian asks.

Elles lisaient ensemble, she says. *Ou sinon, la prière*. Reading or otherwise prayer. Adrian can't recall a single moment where she had expressed faith of any kind. They had never gone to Midnight Mass, had never said grace.

Rosaline-Rosamund was angry about dying, says Dominique, *et elle avait peur*. They see it a lot in their profession, of course. His grandfather, she adds, was the opposite: someone who had their *stratégie de sortie* – exit strategy. But his grandmother was of great help to Rosaline-Rosamund, whatever she did, because eventually *elle a lâchée*, she let go, and was able to die at home. His grandmother, Dominique says as she drains her cup, is *une très belle personne à cause de ça*. She stands up and reaches for his hand. She says then, in heavily accented English: – It is a beautiful thing you are doing, young man. You who are so young.

Then he tries, increasingly, brazenly, to pry into her prehistory. – What made you convert, Nana?

The answers to this question shift like weather.

– When I was in sixth form. There was a new English teacher. Her name was Eileen Jones. She wore red tweed suits.

Or:

– My boyfriend at the time. He was a craftsman. I loved to watch him work.

– Someone lent me Thomas Aquinas. A copy of Thomas Aquinas.

– We read Julian of Norwich.

– St Augustine. Worth listening to what he has to say, you know. He really lived the life before his conversion.

– So fetching, those red tweed suits.

– And when I saw the depths of thought that were in it, that had always been in it, I was hooked.

– When I was little, you see, the Church of England was all rather dry. Catholicism when I encountered it for the first time was exciting.

– Great stagecraft, the Catholics.

– It was the north of England, you see. It was part of our spirit.

When she is long gone, the prosodies of her speech will remain for him: that cool cold confidence, its melodic authority.

– There was the art too, of course.

– The art, Nana?

– Yes. I studied history of art as well. That changed my life. A low dirty chuckle.

She reaches out for an olive. They are drinking Campari with big wedges of lemon on her balcony. The valley is all beneath them. – What about Rome, Nana?

– What about Rome?

– I found something at the house. In the tin box. It said you studied at a place called Regina Mundi.

– What were you doing looking through my papers?

She is like this. The trip-wire of her indignation. The final turn to rage: the mood he must leave her in. He hates it.

– I was looking for a document we need. So you can be here.

Her sneer: Who is *we*?

– You. Me. Mummy.

– Don't fool yourself. This is your project, putting me here. Her finger like a righteous Israelite's on a wall.

– Please, Nana. Don't talk like that.

– I can talk however I damn well please.

There is a long pause in which Adrian considers leaving for ever. He thinks of his friends in London, all of whom work now at private equity firms, or else companies with ugly flagship buildings identifiable from the river. Last time he'd been to London, they spoke about the merits of this or that credit card.

– Regina Mundi closed a few years ago. It was a failed experiment anyway.

– What was?

– All of it. The whole thing. They dangled it in front of us, made us believe we could contribute, that we would be welcomed, and then they whisked it all away. We'd been duped. It was all a purely superficial exercise and we fell for it. They made fools out of all of us.

– I'm afraid I don't follow, Nana.

– Well, try harder then.

– But you haven't even told me what you're talking about. He feels her hauteur stalling on her syntax.

– I am talking about Regina Mundi. It was a place for women. A place we could go, and be together. During the time of the great . . . gathering, it was a good place, a hopeful place.

He knows that if he pushes her, she will tip into the circular sentences from which there is no exit. He is not sure he can do it today. He decides to kiss her and quit it there.
– Wait a minute. I am not finished.
– I know. But I have to go.
– Do you now.
– Yes.

Google yields press clippings. *The National Catholic Reporter*, in June 2005:

> There's some sad news this week with the closing of Regina Mundi, the first center of studies in Rome explicitly created for the theological education of women, and a long symbol of the intellectual coming-of-age of women in the Catholic Church. Regina Mundi marked its fiftieth anniversary just last year.

Financial difficulties. Declining enrolments.

He remembered, intermittently, to bring pleasure to his body too. To that end, he made a habit, every Sunday, of cycling to a spot high upstream in the river gorge, where the water came out from under the rock and was cold and clear. He packed a bag of peaches, and two sandwiches made out of one whole baguette, water. He took off all his clothes, read for a bit, then slept in the mottled shade. Swifts and martens bladed their wingtips in the water. Mosaic-coloured trout snouted against the current. Minnows skitted here and there, like serifs. Now and again frogs of varying sizes leapt from secret ledges and hung in the water, legs lax, with watchful spirit-level eyes.

He let his mind wander to the set of thoughts he felt he was not supposed to think: what was keeping his grandmother, and was there anything he could do to help her die. He felt ill-equipped – no *Dream of Gerontius*, no Latin – that he had grown up outside the traditions which might be useful in this kind of situation. He had no prayers. He didn't know how. His grandmother was walking the perimeter of life, running her hands along it, looking for the exit, the secret sprung panel which would open and release her, and he was powerless to assist her.

Instead he stacks her remaining books into cardboard boxes, a task of several days. It feels like theft. She must know she is never coming back to this house, and he knows she cannot see him doing this, but still: her hurt lurks about the house. It is while he is doing this that he finds the notebook. It falls backwards off the shelf and opens face-down on the floor. When he picks it up, a folded piece of heavy paper slips out. The notebook is filled with her perfect 1960s italics, moving across the pages in adamantine lines. Notes on the Gospels of Matthew and Luke. The paper, though, bears his grandfather's writing: a transcription of 'Air and Angels' by John Donne. His grandfather had added, at the end, 'But John Donne cannot say what first love quickens.' It is undated and unsigned. In another room, the radio is on, coming through a Bluetooth speaker. It is the local public radio for the Bay Area. He likes to listen to the traffic updates, an odd and therefore private pleasure. A jam on 580 northbound. Lane closure on I-80. On the hour they will cut to Lakshmi Sang with the news from Washington. There is a cup of tea cooling on a shelf which he has forgotten all about.

– It's funny, you know, Hilary says on the phone later that night. The first thing Nana asked me to do when he died was to throw away all of his papers.

Adrian is sitting on the sofa. He is turning the notebook over in his hands.

– And I did it without question, Hilary continued. When somebody dies, there is so much . . . admin, and I was just overwhelmed by it all. It killed all my curiosity.

Adrian understands. The list of things he must do for his nana is already so long, and tonight he has forgotten to make himself dinner. What I would not give, he thinks, for someone else to feed me. Just this once. Feed me and afterwards bathe me. Pour warm water over my back.

10

1958

FROM THE TOP deck of the bus, Margaret could see the children playing in the bombed lots which still dotted the length of Kennington Road. Sidings were put up around the skeletal remains of houses; they then had to be demolished, the rubble sorted and cleared. Neat stacks of timber – beams and floorboards – would appear and then disappear periodically. Then it would be bricks: old bricks of London clay, which bore the undulations, like grain in wood, of where they'd been pressed and laid out to dry under other oyster-coloured suns.

She lived in Dorset, a pretty place of thatched roofs and orchards, but she came into London once a week to see Tristan, to whom she tentatively referred, though it felt quite self-aggrandizing, as her lover. She was thirty-one, had been to university, had studied English and French, now worked as a teacher, but it was these forays into London, sitting on the train alone with her sandwiches and her thermos of tea, which made her feel adult, au fait and urbane.

On her day off, she would catch the mid-morning fast service to Paddington, descending immediately into the Underground for Waterloo, watching the eerie exhalations of the upholstery on the Bakerloo line. When she emerged to where the buses congregated, the first thing she was always struck by was the dust. The smell of it hung everywhere, like heavy drapery. It was the dust of ruins and renovation, of the city stirring into the second half of the century. As the foundations of the bombed-out terraces were pulled from the ground like teeth, they disgorged Georgian, Victorian, Edwardian dusts – the dusts of different Englands, which billowed over them and then bedded back into the cells of each and every quickened thing. She felt them shifting there, fighting it out in her lungs.

She had met Tristan when she was home in Sheffield; he'd been doing restoration work on the cathedral. She was home for her father's funeral.

Tristan was working in a temporary masons' yard tucked round the back, on the north side of the nave. The commission was for a series of stiff-leaf carvings for the vaults of a side chapel.

– What plant is that? she'd stopped to ask, her hands thrust deep into the pockets of her trench coat.

– None, he said. They were found only in British architecture, he explained, and didn't seem to represent a real plant. But they naturally follow the movement of the wrists as you make them, he said, holding his up and crossing them. His nails were dirty and there was dust grouting the lines of his palms. There was a copy of St Augustine's *Confessions* in the pocket of his jacket. She asked him, in that forward way she had cultivated since university, if he would like to go for a drink with her when he got off. She motioned towards the book with her chin. Tell me what you think about that, she said.

Afterwards, when the ghosts of their pints had made many overlapping rings on the table, after they had spoken volubly, laughingly, of the Sophist tradition – he had called Aquinas the *bee's knees* and she had confessed, drawing amoebae on the exposed slip of his wrist with her finger, that she had liked that – she slipped from shadow to shadow after him, back to his rented room, past his hawkish landlady. She knew a thing or two about hawkish landladies by then. A good quality for a landlady to have, she had to concede. What was different about this time, with him, was the way her orgasm punched out of her. He put parts of her feet in his mouth. The noise she made was, above all, one of awed surprise. He slipped his hand underneath the back of her head. The other hand was doing something with her leg. All the tendons of her body pulled taut, and then felt long and languorous.

Tristan's studio was in an old stables in Camberwell. There was an outside area where he sometimes worked. He used a metal barrel to heat the space, but it was a matter of finding the fuel for it. He went looking for bits of broken timber in the waste piles of construction sites. His training had been predominantly in the open air, in order to toughen them up – for when you might be winched up into the rafters of a church shortly before Passiontide. He maintained that even outside, he had been warmer than he was now. I am doomed, he said, to develop silicosis and arthritis.

When he'd been a student they'd been encouraged to go looking in bomb sites for anything they could practise on. Their tutor would lead them up the Old Kent Road with wheelbarrows. The cornices or cornerstones of Georgian terraced houses were best, because they were just big enough to be manageable to get back to the studio, and they had often broken away relatively cleanly from the brick in the blasts. If a crust of mortar remained, the challenge was to take it off without taking great chunks out of the stone. He positioned his blocks on a section of old mattress. This he'd also found in a bombed-out house, trapped in a brass bed frame which had been twisted like the ribcage of some mad creature, he said. He'd had to saw the corner off it with a breadknife. Now the Bath stone rocked on the satin blush of it, scattering its chips of silica.

All carvings, he told her, relied on the presumed distance from the viewer. Some of those small medallion faces which you saw halfway up buildings, for instance: if you could get close to them, as he had done (on scaffolding, for days at a time), you could see they were really rough, still bearing many marks of the chisel. Church restoration was the most arduous, he told her, because everything there – no matter how high up or unlit – is there for God, and so it must all be done to a very high finish. He told her that he'd been hired to make six carvings for Southwark Cathedral, and had spent 'weeks just walloping the stone'. They weren't allowed to use drills. All their tools had to be identical to the masons of the Middle Ages. He kept his in a leather roll, which he took home every night under his arm to Oval, where he lived in a small terraced house with his wife and baby.

He told her about his wife the third time they slept together. She couldn't say she was much surprised, but nevertheless she lay very still, as if she had fallen into a grain silo, and would drown if she made to move. The mark of her now would be her passivity to this circumstance. They could not get married. He could not come inside her, and therefore her pleasure was the first imperative. She insisted on it greedily as a point of principle. She did not think she could be a wife in any case. She tried to picture the kind of house this other woman must keep for him, but all she could conjure was a children's dollhouse diorama, lit pinkly by lamps, with a tame fire burning in a tiny grate like a toast rack.

She came round the corner of the mews to his studio and knocked on the textured glass of the door.
– Hello, he said as she came in, and gave her a cup of tea. – Today I will be deepening the shadows on this piece. He motioned to his work stand, where what she'd affectionately nicknamed *The Orgasmic Crocodile* was lying on its side. It featured a naked headless figure, perhaps pregnant, perhaps potbellied, riding a crocodile. The crocodile was curled up at either end, so that its smiling snout reached straight into the air.
He had been born in Rawalpindi, and, when he was eight years old, he told her, he'd been put on a boat from Karachi to Liverpool, via the Suez Canal. It took ten days. There were roughly thirty children, all unaccompanied, all English, all headed for boarding schools. He was being greeted by an aunt he'd never met, in Birmingham. She had told him to stand in the window of the train so that she'd know it was him, but he misunderstood her and had stood all the way from Liverpool, his hands pressed up against the glass, despite his fellow passengers' entreaties. He pissed himself like that, and eventually the tea trolley lady walking through saw the puddle, and offered him a paper napkin.

But he was unlike the other men she'd known to emerge from boarding school: pinched perpetual boys, whose memories of Delhi, Bombay or Nairobi were flooded with the golden light of nostalgia for early childhood, and could never be uncoupled from it. Unlike the others, Tristan gave her a clean feeling. He undressed himself with a quiet self-assurance and hung her shirts considerately on the backs of chairs. His nudity had a matter-of-factness which she liked very much. When they were finished, he would help to do up her hair again, lifting it so that he could get at her back of her neck. No sculptor has ever got this right, he said, running the back of his finger along it. He rocked on the balls of his feet to rinse himself at the sink.

All day she liked to watch him with the bullnose, the deerfoot, the claw chisel. She watched as he made furrows in the stone, chasing the shapes. The rhythmic melodious *puck puck* of the mallet.

Shadows and breath, their affair. That was what made carving, too. He made the music of his tools, and blew away what they left in their wake. He asked for her opinion often. Should I deepen or pierce this shadow? He made her feel the piece he was working on, taking her hand and covering the back of it with his, moving her fingers into the grooves where he wanted the shadows to lie beneath the belly of the crocodile.

This particular afternoon, which was to be, though they didn't know it yet, one of their last, they spoke of the pregnant belly in sculpture: its absence. It was an odd dissonance, they agreed: all through the Renaissance there was fascination with the pregnant body and its workings. Anatomy lectures were bent on its mysteries. Pregnant cadavers were the most sought after, and, consequently, the most expensive. Grave robbers were known to linger beneath the windows of women in labour, listening for the outcome. And pregnancy was such a state of ubiquity and mystery, and of a scale hard to comprehend. Was it merely that it was a thing impossible to carve, without the weight of the belly causing the whole thing to break off? – A pregnant woman sleeping? Margaret suggested. – On her side perhaps? – I will make it for you, he said. One day. Her thoughts flicked, despite her best efforts, to his wife. But he has had a pregnant model in his house, she thought. In painting, they agreed, pregnancy could be seen more often. But in these instances, the pregnancy depicted was offered, instead, as proof of the continuation of a line. These paintings were about property and the safe assurance of its passage; they were portraits of a social order safely repeating itself. The women in these paintings were real, in that they had walked and breathed, but they were not presented as persons, merely as noticeboards of their husbands' wealth.

Motherhood seemed to be a project which now wallpapered the world and seemed to screech at her from every street corner or magazine page; these mothers never pregnant, but ringed with their rotundly headed children, and smiling toothily, anodynely, like hostages. Now and again he would refer to his wife by accident, and then they would both pretend it hadn't happened.

He told her that he loved her hands. They are *so* beautiful, he said, so unusual. Long, like some Northern Renaissance Madonna, or Donatello's Penitent Magdalene. He showed her a photograph plate of it in one of his books. She made a face at him when she saw. No! he said, pointing at the hands.

They were not touching, but leaning towards one another. He explained about carving in wood and the constraints of its grain. How Donatello would have had to burnish the palms of each of her hands. This space, he said, pointing at the gap, making her hands do the same, this space is one of the most erotic in art.

They were in the plausibly deniable margin of the day now, when his wife would be warming the oven, and if he was a little late, it was only a minor, though cumulative, irritation. He turned the electric lights off, lighting the candle on the windowsill. His day with Margaret was ending.

He came over to her then, and slid his hand up her skirt very slowly. He undid the popper on her garter, and peeled off her thick brown stocking, which he flung dramatically over his shoulder. He circled his thumb round the nub of her ankle bone, with his other hand he lifted the cup out of her hands.

They did not speak of the future, because there could not be one.

11

THEN HER MOTHER died.

She came home from work one evening and her landlady was waiting by the phone.

Her father had been dead six months. She hadn't been able to visit much since the funeral.

His death had been a long time coming: a second heart attack. After the first, when he'd been in hospital, he'd developed a liking for *The Archers*, and thereafter insisted on playing it through the kitchen window while he gardened.

The thing which killed her mother was also a kind of heart attack. A rupture, the doctor told her. Like a rip. A big red ripping of the left ventricle, while she was doing the Saturday crossword.

While she was away she did not speak to Tristan.

Upon her return to London, he told her he'd been offered work on the reconstruction of Exeter Cathedral. They were walking along the North Embankment, towards Parliament, and there was a slow rain. He was telling her that it would be a long assignment, perhaps as much as a year. He could move his family (she hadn't heard him call them that before) there, and let the house. He said that his wife was pregnant again. Margaret's attention was caught by a swan flying over a double decker bus on Westminster Bridge. There was a dull feeling in her chest, vectored by the sense that this was where they had always been headed. Even as he tried to hold her hand, his eyes were wide with anticipatory pleasure. She kissed him glassily and wished him a long vocation of such excitements, then opened her umbrella emphatically, defensively, and brought it down low over her face in order to cry as she walked away from him, back towards Temple. She pulled a glove off angrily with her teeth, wiping ineffectually at her eyes. Back in her bedsit she sat in her cold cream-coloured room, on the edge of her bed with its coverlet of peach crochet, and felt indelibly lonely.

At Christmas her school friend Nicole phoned and suggested Margaret come stay with Nicole's parents. The invitation came from them too, she assured her. She was emphatic on this point. – For the festive period, she said, but also beyond. She meant while Margaret packed up her own parents' house. Margaret accepted. She gave notice at her job and to her landlady, packed her suitcase, and boarded the train back to Sheffield. All the way she looked out of the window. Watched the northern hills gather their shapes. Resisted thinking of him.

She knew Nicole from Our Lady Immaculate College of Mexborough. Her first day there aged sixteen, she saw the statue of Mary at the foot of the main staircase and her interest was immediate. When her parents had taken her to church, it was habitual. They sang the songs and went home to a roast. And Jesus presided, and the interior was plain, painted in various shades of custard. But Mary was dressed in red and a deep, weathered blue, and Margaret found her much more interesting than her son. THE MARIAN CULT = MUCH MORE COMPELLING, she had written in her diary at the time.

Nicole came from a Catholic family. Her mother seemed pregnant for all of their years together at school. One day the two girls were walking down the street, discussing *The Mill on the Floss*, when one of Nicole's older sisters met them on the pavement about eighty yards from their front door. – Um, she began, rushed. Mummy's not well, and . . .

Here they craned around her to see that Nicole's mother was, in fact, strapped to a stretcher and being loaded onto the back of a horse-drawn ambulance. Nicole looked at her sister with eyes blazing.

The sister's lip started to quiver, because what did any of them know, really.

Apparently their mother had ignored the most recent baby while it screamed. Then she had started to scream, and she had not stopped.

She was gone for a week. When she came back, her hair was dirty, but Nicole and her sister were relieved to see that she held the new baby brother without incident, and their father still kissed her on the top of her head when he came home in the evenings.

Nicole's father was a mild man. Margaret had always liked him.

He waited for her on the station platform now, wearing tweed which looked as if it had been cut from the turf. – Hello, dear, he said paternally into her temple, as they kissed each other's cheeks. He'd put the spare car rug on the front seat for her, and there was a tubular tin of ginger biscuits.

There had been a frost since November, and it persisted, vitreous, in the shadows cast by the spread oaks and the drystone walls as they came over the hills and towards the house. It was a beautiful house, freestanding at the end of a residential street, and looked at this moment much like a Christmas card. Red and orange rosehips bobbed brightly against the windows, under the weight of a senatorial robin, who flitted from one branch to the next. Nicole emerged on the doorstep to wave excitedly. Margaret got out of the car.

That first Christmas of being an orphan, it was the company of Nicole's family which appealed to her. Nicole's mother seemed to be done with babies. There were twelve of them in total, the eldest now thirty-seven, and well into the childbearing of her own, the youngest only nineteen. They joked that they had to eat in shifts, buying whole fishes and roasting them with the oven door open and the tray resting on it: first the tail end, then the other. They turned out great troughs of roast potatoes and formed orderly lines to make Staffordshire oatcakes. The kitchen table was lined on either side with benches. The house was laced with the smells of life taking place: wet wool, dog, pipe smoke, laundry drying, pastry.

Margaret was sharing a room with Nicole's sisters. Nicole was married now, but she still lived nearby, and over that week or so in which Margaret stayed, Nicole came over and spent whole days cooking with all of them. It was novel for Margaret, an only child, to have so many people around. She felt they reasserted the lines of herself. On Christmas Eve they went to Midnight Mass, the mud room was rummaged in and a spare pair of rubber boots found for Margaret, and a selection of hats and mittens for her to choose from. It was snowing heavily, and Nicole held Margaret's hand inside her coat pocket as they headed into the village. The nativity play had real animals and a screaming, puce-coloured baby. Margaret ran her fingers along the carved pew-end, where a feathered beast spread itself. When they stood to sing, she let her attention wander over the pediments and the arches and the places where the grouting in the stonework showed, and she felt a tide swell within herself, a surge of love for the communing creatureliness of it all. Beside her, Nicole's mouth made the perfect O of *yon*.

On Boxing Day, the whole family went for a long walk, and Nicole and Margaret dropped behind. They reminisced about their English teacher, Eileen Jones.

– I wrote an essay on Gawain, do you remember? Margaret said. I said something about the 'Dark Ages'.

– Ah yes, that was a bugbear of hers, wasn't it! said Nicole brightly.

The Middle Ages! was Eileen Jones's red reply. *My beloved Middle Ages, Margaret.*

The manner Eileen Jones had of walking into a classroom. The soft *pock* of the chalk as it made contact with the board. The text on their desks was *Tess*. Eileen Jones lent Margaret copies of Thomas Aquinas and Julian of Norwich. They gave new high-water marks to her mind. – And she said we could call her by her first name. And do you remember when she took us to the pub, on V.E. Day? Nicole swung their recollections round into another direction. Margaret felt Nicole's hand at the crook of her arm. She tipped her head up and looked at the oaks spread out like the ceiling of a master mason. It was the first day when she'd thought of Tristan not at all.

V.E. Day had been the first day of their exams. When Margaret did well in them, Eileen suggested she apply to Oxford.

She went. Her room at Lady Margaret Hall looked out over the garden and the punts moored on the river; she studied English and French. She read *The Dream of the Rood* in bed, the bricks at the bottom of her heater giving off the last dregs of their heat. She went to the Ashmolean and stood for long minutes in front of Uccello's *The Hunt in the Forest*; thought, indeed, of the forest as a force which pulsed on the edges of the mapped world through the centuries, how we had tamed our forests now, made them without mystery, felled them for profit.

Oxford at that time was in a state of flux. The student body was a confused mix between those, like Margaret, who'd grown up with the war, whose coming-of-age coincided neatly with its end; and ex-service people who'd interrupted their studies to join. For the women's colleges in particular, this posed a problem: there was a curfew, but many of the older women, ex-Navy or former nurses, disregarded it flagrantly, and of course this had its influence on the younger students. You weren't supposed to have male visitors, but they did, and sometimes they stayed all night, or neighbours from Margaret's staircase were out all night. She saw them, smoking vehemently, outside the office where they were given a talking-to, grinding their cigarette butts angrily into the cobbles with the sole of a shoe. In the end the college gave up; there was a loose double standard and a performance of discipline for younger students who followed the lead of the older. Margaret got good at climbing through windows into the male colleges and climbing back out at dawn. She learnt to smoke, drink port.

Most of the boys her age had been to Harrow or Eton or Winchester, their fathers were KCs or MPs or peers. When she told them that her father was an engineer, they sneered. They wrong-footed her, with their performed anti-intellectualism and airs of sexual belittlement. They were lewd, and taken aback when she was lewd in kind. These younger men had not been in the war, and they were perpetually enraged by it, and took it out on the women. She learnt to avoid them altogether. The older men, those who had come back from France or Egypt or Burma, took notice; they wanted her youth and her innocence. And she gave it them, willingly.

She slept with men because she wanted to get good at sleeping with them. For all their pretensions – they read Lawrence – the younger ones were mostly bad at it, and always would be. Their educations had permanently cramped them, they were cut back, like bonsai trees. When they climaxed, it was with small noises of shame, and then they lay there, not knowing what to do next. If they fell asleep, she snuck out. The older ones were nonplussed about their bodies, about scars or sites of pain, in a way which drew her to them. Sex with them was perfunctory, not tentative, and she preferred it. They were matter-of-fact, pulling the sheaths off with that soft snap afterwards and letting them fall to the floor.

She covered her face with her hands when – if – she came.

The unsanctified aspects of sex interested her. She liked the smooth of certain skins against her mouth. The smell in the crease of an elbow, the back of the knee, the hip. Taking an Achilles tendon, gently, between the teeth. To feel it all at the base of her brain. She held them as they came, shaking.

Some of them were arrestingly, atypically beautiful, but evidently had no idea what to do about it. They lay in bed of a fifth-week afternoon telling her at length about Cicero and the politics of the Late Roman Republic. She found there was something deeply erotic in this: when they were without shame in their minds' delights. She would get dressed and walk away under the fan arches of their colleges, sincerely wishing them a lifetime of these enthusiasms. May you always be brought low by the Horatian odes, she wished them; may you for ever weep at Hector and Andromache, with Astyanax in their arms. Of course, it was all in vain. These men would be appearing in the papers years hence, for some fault of policy, in their suits of black and grey, looking pursed, their hair thinning. They would have sons they never touched, and studies whose doors were for ever shut, and so the cycle would begin again. When she thought on this too long, she had a feeling like a wall of rock descending. What use was she, with her breasts and education? She thought of all the married women she knew, and shuddered at their wings clipped by their wedded lives. What had she imagined, ultimately, for herself and Tristan? She could not say.

She caught Nicole's eyes searching her face. They had arrived at a pub so picturesque it could be an advent calendar. Inside, Margaret could make out members of Nicole's extended family standing under the low brown beams. Nicole squeezed her arm. They went in.

And when she was asked, in the gloaming of her life, what started it, Catholicism, what was the answer? Had she been sixteen, or twenty-nine? What kind of room had it happened in? And had it been Eileen's copy of Thomas Aquinas, or this family which had gathered her up into its arms when she was alone and flailing, or was it the man who put her toes in his mouth, in Camberwell candlelight, when gardens had begun to grow in the craters of Peckham, Brockley, Canada Water and New Cross Gate?

12

AFTER THAT FIRST Christmas with Nicole and her family, Margaret moved back to Mexborough. She wrote to Eileen, asking if there were any vacancies at Our Lady Immaculate and, to her delight, Eileen, by then head of the English department, said there was one, and that she'd love to hire her as a colleague. She then paid Margaret the great compliment of asking her for her opinion on redrafting the traditional syllabus.

– I want to shake up all the old guard, Margaret, she said. Our business is educating conscientious young women. They spent nights in the pub, piecing together sequences of texts: *Tess*, *The Tempest*, *Jane Eyre*, *The Wife of Bath*, *Frankenstein*, Elizabeth Barrett Browning, T. S. Eliot, Waugh.

– Education, said Eileen, eloquently drunk, emphatic circles of cigarette, is the unfolding of souls. It is like love in that regard.

For a year, Margaret marked the high holy days with Nicole and her family. By Ascension, she had decided to convert.

It was a way of being *with them*, she would say, many years hence, to someone as yet unconceived.

Catholicism gave back to her the concept of daily life. It was the master discourse moving through all things. It was one thing happening after one another, manageably: Advent, Lent, Easter.

In the meantime, she had inherited a little money from her parents. The horizons of her world lifted and hovered, waiting to be rearranged.

Her friends began having children. Falling pregnant, she phrased it to Eileen when they went to the pub. Eileen listened, with her red mouth and sleek tweed suits, steadfast Eileen with her assessing eyes and sharp laugh. Eileen who lived discreetly in a central Sheffield flat with a woman called Carol, an archivist for the city council. There was something in her friends' contentment which she despised, Margaret told Eileen, and Eileen nodded slowly, calmingly. Once they'd had the babies, they could never meet in the centre of town any more, and Margaret had instead to trek out to the suburbs, in her comfortable but ugly shoes. Here, on these residential streets with their uniform houses, their bland gardens full of meaty red roses, she felt herself to be in hostile territory. The breezy tone her friends employed, when she talked about books she'd been enjoying recently, to say that they never had time to read any more, in fact, they couldn't remember the last book they'd read. The queenly way they moved, like ships. The witchiness with which they spoke to one another's children, or dandied fingers in their faces.

Nicole had impressed them both, when she got pregnant, newly wed, by stepping into motherhood as into some noble and dignified role in industry. And when little Martha came, Margaret saw in Nicole a split consciousness appear. She could be at Nicole's kitchen table, sipping tea, telling her about travails in her teaching, and Nicole would be nodding, while folding miniscule items of clothing, or making porridge on the stove with the baby on her hip. She modulated her speech for the baby: a voice Margaret didn't know. Always there appeared to be something ticking beneath Nicole's skin: the sorting of tasks into an order that stretched ahead and filled the hours.

It never occurred to Margaret to offer to hold the baby while Nicole did these things.

Nicole fell pregnant again, and proclaimed that she wanted Margaret to think of herself as an aunt. Nicole and her sisters, she told Margaret, were often tetchy with one another, vying to out-domesticate each other.

Margaret sat and knitted with Nicole pregnant, each woman making one half of a pair of booties. When the baby arrived – a second girl – she brought herself to the task. She found the baby ugly, with her crinkled red face and drooping lip. Her hands looked like hermit crabs on the ends of her arms. When the dust of the world snagged in the baby's nostrils and crusted there, Margaret felt a deep disgust. She found the piles of milk-coagulated muslin repulsive, too, and took to subtly breathing through her mouth when she was at Nicole's house.

But she paid more attention than she had the first time round.

As the months flicked by, Martha began talking, and the new one's features rounded out, and Margaret found that they were quite fun, and she was good with them. When she went to visit Nicole now, Martha would hurtle down the hall towards her and demand to be taken into the garden, where she, stomping arrhythmically, led Margaret by the hand, pointing out flowers and bees.

Then the baby started crawling, at speed, and this necessitated scooping her out of harm's way, quickly and elegantly. Margaret learnt that it came very naturally, to find where to place one's hands on the baby's ribcage, how much pressure to exert in the hold, how to lift the baby and use the momentum of the lift to your own advantage, bringing the baby in to face you and resting it on your torso. To her surprise, she liked this. She started to kiss the baby, surreptitiously at first, on the back of her head or in the hollow at the nape of her neck, where the smell was thickest; then with great pantomime gusto, because this made the baby laugh and the baby's laugh brought pure, iridescent joy in Margaret's chest. Soon she was covering the baby's head in kisses, and her hands, and the soles of her feet. She abandoned herself to it. When she said goodbye to Nicole after an afternoon of this, she clasped her friend hard and smoothed her back. Her life, entirely her own but punctuated by hours like these, pockets of time spent in absorption, a sense of wonder loaned to her, were some of her happiest.

Then one day she caught Nicole looking at her stonily, as she lifted her head from blowing raspberries on the baby's belly. Margaret saw immediately that Nicole had been caught out, had never intended for her to see her gaze like that. Nicole rearranged her face, lowering the curtain of a wan, conciliatory smile. Margaret was stilled, slightly stunned, one of the baby's wrists in each hand as she knelt on the rug; she reached up and dabbed at her mouth with the back of a hand self-consciously. Nicole offered her another cup of tea, her voice bearing a forced brightness. Margaret recognized she was being graciously offered an opportunity to leave, so declined, picking her handbag off the back of a chair and clutching it awkwardly to her chest, swiping her jacket from the coat hook in the hall and letting herself out a little too quickly, while Nicole followed her out slowly, calling ahead something about next week, but Margaret's ears were pulsing hotly and she didn't hear. On the bus home she kept her bag pressed to her ribs and felt queasy. She tried to look outside the window, but every time the bus brushed through the low-hanging branches of plane trees, she felt their knock as an unpleasant vibratory twinge in her inner ear. The air was muggy and laced with smog; she took shallow breaths of it and resolutely pushed it out through her nostrils, but it gave her no peace. The baby's giggles, combined with the hot sensation of Nicole's apprehended glance, curdled within her.

The next time she saw Eileen, she allowed her head to loll melodramatically in her hands at the pub table as she recounted it. Eileen offered nothing and instead asked her if she'd decided what to do yet with her inheritance. Then she told her she could go to Rome. There was a college there, brand new, it had only opened in 1954, the smell of fresh paint still on its walls, where women – not just any women, but laywomen – could study theology, could train to teach it. This, Eileen told her, was almost unprecedented in human history. Practically only Heloise (of Abelard fame) could possibly lay claim to something remotely similar, Eileen said, waving her hands. She snaked a brochure between the beer mats to her.

Its name was Regina Mundi.

A few months later, Margaret requested and received the appropriate forms, filled them out and returned them, was accepted, and went to the travel agent to buy her tickets. She asked Nicole if she would house some of her parents' furniture. The day she said goodbye to her, she resisted her friend's entreaties to come inside for tea, Nicole had made a ginger cake specially. It was true, Margaret could smell it. But Margaret claimed she had errands to run; she clasped her hands in front of her in a show of resolute efficiency. Martha stood staring in the living-room window, sucking her thumb and playing with the lace curtain, pressing a plump jammy hand up against the glass. Margaret tried not to look at her, didn't wave, and clipped back down the garden path in what she hoped was a picture of self-possession. Really she was blinkered by her own tears, her love for Martha, she felt, violently delegitimized, and now she had nowhere to put it. It sloshed and soured inside her.

Nicole shut the front door before she'd reached the street.

13

2019

THERE WAS A painting his nana wanted him to get for her from the house. – It's blue, she kept saying. She was braced against the arms of her chair, as if she thought she might fall out of it. – He loved it. I want it with me. Will you get it for me. Then the absolute rarity: – Please. Please will you get it for me.

– Nana, I don't know what you're talking about.

– It's *blue*. She was laboured now, her breath coming hard and trochaic. – Shades of *blue*.

He called his mother to ask what she thought his grandmother could be talking about.

– Oh, said Hilary. Look in the attic. It was a painting they had in their bedroom when I was growing up. When he died she asked me to put it away. It's quite big. You'd have to take it to her on the bus or something.

It was square. Some sort of head and shoulders Madonna and Child. Sure enough, all in shades of blue. Of its time, that stylized 1960s sensibility of flattened shapes making figures. The cheek of the Christchild a shallow domed disc, a helmety bowl cut. The Virgin's drapery like interlocking scythes, dotted with the sharp cut-out shapes of stars.

– I brought you that painting you asked for, Nana.
Her look turning to him like an empty room.
– What painting?
He unwrapped it from the blanket he'd brought it in.
– The Madonna and Child.
– Oh that. Some strings pulled taut behind her eyes. – It's not, you know. It's Jesus and Joseph.
Then he watched as she leapt like a swimmer into this sudden current of thought. She began telling him, animatedly, clearly, her back straight as a plinth, how she always thought Joseph was a figure who never really got his due.
– There are so many scholars doing interesting things now in the field of the historical Jesus, she said. And some have suggested that Mary's pregnancy was a result of rape, which would have left her ostracized. But Joseph does the kindly thing, and says he'll marry her, and that it doesn't matter. We never really know how old Joseph is, you know. He could be much older. But he looks after her. And even if they all believed in the immaculate conception theory, how do you think that would make him feel? She laughed: the flinty flash of mischief in her eyes.
– He is cuckolded by God!
He asked her where the painting had come from. He watched as she gathered all her lucidity into her fists.
– It was a sample for a big commission he was going to make.

– Who?

– When he was at St Joseph's. He wanted to fill the church with frescoes like that, all in shades of blue. He had such plans, you see. We both did.

Adrian offered: I like how modern it is. She mmmed in agreement.

– It was one of the few things he was able to take with him, when they threw him out. That painting. He was never even allowed back into the building. He had to leave everything, all his vestments which he'd saved up for over the years. Some his mother had embroidered for him. They were so splendid, you know. Some of the things priests wear can be so gaudy, but his were gorgeous. Plum and pomegranate colours. Greens you would not believe. Sumptuous. They didn't even let him clear out his office. He had that painting at the house because he had wanted to show it to me. He cut the canvas off the frame with a penknife and rolled it up for me so I could keep it safe for him. He was worried they would want to search the house to make sure he didn't take anything with him. Any evidence of what he'd been . . . before.

Adrian sat very still, as if sudden movement might dispel her willingness to tell him any more.

– Where would you like me to put it, Nana?

– Somewhere I can see it all the time. Please. She was pensive and spoke slowly, but it was a self-assured slowness. Her chin was resting on the curl of her hand.

While he hung it on the hook available, she said to his back:

– When our baby came, he wanted to hold her all the

time, you know. It was most unusual in a man of our generation.

Adrian took longer than was necessary to check the frame was hanging level.

– He was a rare person.

14

1960

ON HER FIRST day in Rome Margaret had the most delicious meal of her life: gnocchi con vongole e fiori di zucca. It was a near-rapturous experience, and she giggled to herself, hoping it would be tenable to live at such a pitch.

She wanted to plunge down every street.

The absolute luxury of being a woman alone.

One of the first things she did was to visit the Church of the Gesú, which Eileen had recommended to her, in that emphatic manner of hers. It was known for its trompe l'oeil ceiling, depicting the rings of paradise. Dante's vision dolled up in the glad rags of the baroque, she had said. When Margaret arrived, having got lost, it was late afternoon. Light was lancing the dusty crystals of the chandeliers. She had lain down on a pew at the back to look up, moving slowly so as not to attract attention to herself. She had planned on doing this, and had worn a long skirt on purpose. She smoothed its pleats over her thighs and crossed her ankles. Saints and kings cavorted on concentric cornices of sorbet-coloured cloud. Heaven looked a riot. Popes and bishops blessed those down below, their tiaras cocked by the celestial breeze. Life-size statues of angels dangled into the space, just pairs of legs and wingtips, the rest of their bodies bursting into glorious shades of pink and peach on the painted panel. The billows of its clouds spilled beyond the frame like fleece over the ceiling's coffers. Angels lithe and lissome kicked their feet and clasped their hands. The pew's narrowness dug into her back. She felt languid like an animal and recalled Eileen's report on her from school: *Margaret has a feline tendency to luxuriate on a Friday afternoon.* She must have spent twenty minutes like that, her eyes slowly moving round the ceiling, until a deacon emerged from the vestry, and became flustered, saying, *Signora, por favore!* again and again until she was out of the building and the door had been shut behind her emphatically.

Next in the order of business was to see some Berninis. *Apollo and Daphne* in the Villa Borghese; and, of course, Saint Teresa. Eileen had shown them these, too, but had issued a caution before she changed the slides. They gasped and laughed – if one of the sisters had come in then – and did their looking quickly. She'd imagined the sculptures for years, having only seen them printed in the granulated greys of guidebooks. She walked to the Galleria Borghese all the way from Trastevere. As she arrived, the light was that flat, hyperreal gold of late afternoon in the northern Mediterranean, the light which banks hard upon strong sudden summer rain. It shone on every leaf and made them sharp and flat against clouds of lustrous Prussian grey, as if they were trapped inside a photographic negative, the silver nitrate pooling, after the flash. She bought a ticket at the kiosk for final entry. Already the crowds of tourists were spilling out onto the gravel drive, stunned and starting off in search of food, their evenings beginning. She fought the current descending the stairs.

First, *The Rape of Proserpina*. That godhand dimpling the thigh flesh. It was the first thing you saw when you came up the spiral staircase. She felt unready. She walked around it slowly, unconscious of the fact that she was holding her breath. Her hands were clasped before her, over the handle of her bag. Her toes were tender in her shoes. The room's other elements intruded as if they were noise: the chatter of the marbled ceiling, and the relief sculptures round its edges whispering. She did her best to push them away. There were thin blinds pulled down low over the windows. Outside she could just detect the contrast between the gold, the grey and the green. She made her way around the rooms slowly, placing each foot before the other silently, like a hunter tracking. There was Caravaggio's *Boy with a Basket of Fruit*, which she didn't know would be there, and which she paced in front of, seeing how the light shone off the sateen surface of the black. There was Bernini's *David*. At this she had a sharp intake of breath, uncontrolled and unforeseen. He was ever so slightly smaller than life size, his head level with hers. He was taking his aim. He was biting his lip! There was a glimpse of scrotum behind the drapery, and the segment of cock on top of it. She was taken aback, in general, to find the level of finish on the penises, how many of the foreskins had been drilled up into. She loved the bodies of the middle-aged gods, how they were thick-set but fit, sometimes the thrill at their intricately carved pubic hair. She gasped aloud at the light shining through a marble fold of cloth.

Then on to the Santa Maria della Vittoria for Saint Teresa.

The church was in fact very small, and set off a busy roundabout. The statue itself was off to one side, almost inscrutable in the dingy light. The windows behind it were dirty, and the day was overcast. It was also positioned slightly higher than she was expecting, so that Teresa's ecstasy, which had been unmistakeable in the slides shown in that attic, some Friday in 1944, was in fact invisible to someone of her height or less. Margaret smiled ruefully at Bernini's cunning in the scented dark. There was a discreet coin slot positioned to the left, near the balustrade, where a few lira would turn on a set of weak spotlights for ten minutes.

Opposite the statue, the wax-encased remains of Santa Vittoria leered out at her, her sarcophagus windowed along one side and lit by a moth-mottled strip of halogen: the casing over her hands split, revealing the crumbling stuff beneath. Her teeth looked strange too, inside her slightly open mouth – gappy, like a cemetery suffering from subsidence. She had smooth rounded breasts, and a wound at her neck, with delicately painted drips of blood emerging from it. Her hair was honey blonde, and curled in ringlets like a doll's.

In Santa Cecilia, a marble statue of the saint lay under the altar. The body was draped, contorted, the gash at the neck exposed. The winding sheet clung to her thighs. Margaret was interested in the virgin martyrs, Saints Agnes, Agatha, Lucy, Barbara. These women had often done little more than resist marriage to non-Christians, and, in return, had been beheaded (it seemed this was the preferred mode of killing a virgin). Occasionally, there were stories in the Catholic papers about more recent virgin martyrs: many of them Polish, the overwhelming majority of them women who had resisted sexual advances and then been murdered for it, their bodies cut into pieces and found in ditches.

After a week or so, when she had had a chance to familiarize herself with the college and her timetable, she went to the laundry. The supplicants had to work in it, a couple of hours a week, and they stood alongside the hired women, whose forearms bulged under their rolled sleeves. Margaret asked to be added to the rota. The mother superior thought it a strange request.
– But you are a laywoman.
– I thought it might help me with my Italian, Sister.
– I don't know why you'd be wanting to be learning *their* Italian, Miss Bendelow.
She had only her history of art vocabulary: sfumato, chiaroscuro, impasto.
– Can I at least try?
– Suit yourself.
Every Tuesday morning, she spent three hours in that room. She loved the expanses of white which filled it, the sheets hanging from the racks on pulleys and the women's muscles swelling like sailors' when they pulled them up or down, the wet slap sounds of water in the tubs, the sibilance of brushes, dozens, scrubbing together. She liked the women's talk, how it rose and fell, its enervations. She was habituating her ear to them. They were a great mix of ages, some as young as sixteen, others well into their sixties. At first they humoured her, taught her terms for things they could lay their hands on: soap, mangle, peg. One week an older woman said something obviously salacious, given the

expression on a younger one's face, and the way she glanced over at Margaret. Margaret saw the older one smile. She motioned to Margaret, drew a circle round her face, brought her hands together in prayer, and shook her head. Margaret laughed. They spoke no English, so it was up to Margaret to make a fool of herself with the blunt edges of her Italian. They were encouraging, laughing at her mistakes and congratulating her when she got her Rs just right.

One day, a younger laundress came in timidly turning a ring on her finger, and the others crowded round her, all speaking over each other. There were hand gestures. Giving advice of a certain nature, she supposed. She hung back. Weeks later, the young woman came back in with a stack of folded linens in her arms. The others crowded round her, solicitous and excited on her behalf. One by one the linens were unfolded to reveal initials, embroidered in a style which dated them to the Art Deco period. 'Her mother's mother's mother,' said one of the women, turning back to Margaret explanatorily, gesturing at them. Her mother had kept them, the young woman said, for her marriage. They needed to be washed and pressed afresh. Margaret reached out to feel one. It was woven from linen of a heavy grain, cool to the touch. The initials – a long-dead woman's future married name – were embroidered in a variety of stitches. Not so long ago, young women would still have made these things by hand, all through their late teens, leaving the space for monograms blank and then finishing them when they knew the names of their betrotheds. Then these pieces – and they were complemented with nightgowns, bloomers, shifts, pillowcases – were folded and packed into chests. For centuries women had done this, and it was the only thing which went with them into the terra incognita of their marriages. With men they knew so little of. What kind of husbands would they be to them? Where would married life take them? Would they bleed to death on these sheets, after the nth child or almost-child? And now women did this no more. Instead they passed these heirlooms on, from beyond death like blank maps, encoded documents whose information was no longer accessible, offering some comfort to their female descendants, who had to chart each new bed afresh, alone. Margaret thought of Tristan, then tried not to.

The women worked together to wash and press the inherited sheets, incorporating them seamlessly into the day's load, and each one treated them as if they were her own inheritance. By the end of the day, the stack had been remade, crisped with starch, wrapped in tissue paper and tied with string, and the young woman deposited it in the basket of her bicycle, and cycled home to cheers from the older women on the steps.

Margaret supposed this is what women had always done, when left alone with cloth-based tasks to hand. Knitting. Darning. Weaving. Washing. They gathered, and because of their place in a world of men, the men left them to it. And so it was that they were free, then: to speak at last among themselves. Unattended and uncontrolled. She was standing in the blank space of history. All around her, the damp laundry exuded its semen-smell. This place was deemed an absence, a non-place where nothing of consequence occurred; but that was wrong. It was a rich space, of strength, where women taught each other things. When she plunged her arms up to her elbows into the milky water, when she rubbed salve into her chapped hands, when she saw the other women smiling to each other over the troughs, she felt a muscle memory stirring.

Near sunrise on another day: she stumbled into the Campo de' Fiori. There was a smell of clean wetness, freshly cut greens. She wandered among the stalls in amazement at the variety of leaves. She stopped at a stall heaped high with curled radicchio, pink leaves with their folds and flecks, butter lettuces, boots of cavolo nero tied with twine, dandelion leaves and rocket in stacked baskets. Of course, she didn't know their names then, or what to do with them. A stallholder humoured her. Cavolo nero, he said, you chopped and fried with garlic and chilli. Garlic was the other thing: a key part of that initial rapture, she now knew. The symphonic warmth in that first mouthful of sauce, like an orchestra warming its strings. The water from the flower buckets ran clean and cold, smitten with petals, over the cobbles.

She woke early again and again, and walked along the river, under the gulls. She learnt to drink coffee. She learnt to choose fruit by smelling it. She learnt to sleep during the afternoon, and stay up later at night. She watched the price of cherries drop by the day and then bought a kilo at a time, sharing them out among the sisters. After a few months, the churches began to swim together.

When she passed the shops where clerical garb was sold, she often made accidental eye contact with the saleswomen within. These women wore all black, skirt suits with stilettos, the stockings with the line up the back. They had measuring tapes round their necks. Margaret wondered how that worked. Did you make an appointment? How did you choose? Surely there must be a list.

A set of vestments arrived in the laundry one day. The woman who untied the bundle sprang back when she saw what was inside. The chasuble slipped out and slid onto the floor. It was jewel-coloured, jacquard, Margaret could see, with a pattern of artichokes. There was metalwork embroidery, down the sides, and some beading. Quickly the most senior washerwoman was called over, to take it on. Margaret watched as she laid the garment flat on a worktable, filled a small basin with the mildest water, got out a fresh bar of soap from a box high on a shelf, lined with glassine paper, then spread the chasuble over her knees and dabbed at the stains with a damp cloth, working soap into them. Once she had done this, she took the vestments outside into the courtyard and laid them flat on a rack in the sun, until the soap caked. Then she brought everything back inside and rinsed it all slowly, and repeated the process. It took her all day.

They had lessons on the liturgy, dogmatics, catechetics and the history of Western theology. She took extension classes in Old Hebrew, Ancient Greek and Latin. She felt the thrill of it all: descending into the etymology of words in each language as if into a dig, bearing her clutch of fine-hair brushes, paring back the sand of centuries, grain by grain. She loved the Greek Septuagint most of all, its sexful mouthfeel, each letter a thing of etched and laboured beauty.

The women came from all over the world: Calcutta, Québec, Tennessee. The first thing she noticed was the variety of wimples. There were double-horned cornets which looked like pastries, and stiff box-like shapes which made her think of Tudor women, and softer veils which hung suspended on the wake of their own passage. In their class photo, Margaret was the only one not in a habit.

A group of them rode the bus together.

– Don't imagine, Sister Julian told her, leaning in as they passed the Colosseum, that this habit gives you any more protections from getting your bottom pinched.

They went to late-night masses and the more daring followed these up with drinks in basement bars, where Margaret tasted Aurum for the first time. Sister Marcella introduced her to it. Sister Helen didn't like it. Margaret drank hers for her.

Or they went back to their rooms, and stayed up late at night, drinking cocoa and talking. Some of the other women were young, like her, and others older, on sabbatical from their orders, the apples of their cheeks still full, and their eyes bright. Some of them had wicked senses of humour which came in unnerving barracuda flashes. She loved sitting with them at the long tables of the refectory; the quick, efficient way they made their way down corridors. When she thought of Regina Mundi, later in life, it was always, in fact, a vision of some longitudinal space: the dining hall, the corridor, the narrow lengths of their beds.

They ate lentils in deep wide plates with diaphanous discs of radish, or else stew with blanched knucklebones or pieces of oxtail, or white fish with tomatoes and capers and black olives. She felt her palate shifting, moving to meet the stronger flavours of this place.

❖

The time is of great consequence. She makes friends, easily. Sister Frances, a small, spry woman with exquisitely formed eyebrows, who came from one of the Carolinas, with whom she travelled to Florence and Siena and Milan. But also Giovanni, from Tuscany, whom she met in a bar, and together they spoke of how the Church had too little regard for the other creatures of the world. He was a seminarian, but he would later abandon his training after his deaconate and never get to full priesthood. He would instead join his brother back on the family farm and thereafter send her jugs of olive oil every winter for the rest of his life (it gave off its agate light). *Ecco il mio posto*, he will tell her as they walk his land in the warm twilight of their lives. Here is my place. He will ultimately be known for his writings on sustainable agriculture. All of God's intentions for us and Creation, he will say, can be summed up in two words from Genesis: 'keep it'.

It was all of a piece: the cuts of meat curing in the restaurant windows, the busty saints encased in wax, the *vongole*, the lingerie mannequins. The ecstatic martyrdom of the *fiori di zucca*, the *fior di latte*, the *frutti di bosco*. It was every passing pleasure, every pleasure passing; for ever and ever.

In the summer term of their first year she took a weekend trip with Sister Frances to Florence to see Michelangelo's *David*. They caught the train on a Friday afternoon, as soon as classes finished for the day, pulling into Santa Maria Novella at the cusp of the summer dusk. They rushed to their pensione and dropped their suitcases off before hurrying back out to get to the Galleria dell'Accademia. They were among the last group of visitors admitted for the day. It was quiet inside, a thin crowd, she could hear the sandal-slapped street outside as other tourists went in search of aperitivi.

The two of them rounded the corner into the long corridor, at the top of which he stood in his custom-built alcove, and the breath fell out of her. She remembered the first time she had seen a picture of him. Eileen had shown them. This was another of her illicit, split-second slides, up in the attic, and the fervent hope of no administrative interruptions from Sister Dorothy (they were thankful for the creaking stair). 'I of course am not allowed to say this, girls, but he really is *the* David,' Eileen had said in warning, and clicked it through. The sight of him trilled each end of her ribs. She felt the hair on her knuckles rise up. His furrow of frown! The orderly curls of his hair!

She proceeded to walk up the corridor towards the statue two or three steps at a time. She was watching what it felt for him to be so far away and less above her, and then his increasing closeness, his height, the vertiginous sensation of him over them. When she reached the top she hung back from the other visitors, who went as close as they could, craning and contorting their necks. She walked slowly round the pedestal, examining him from every angle. Those enormous, flawed hands and that preposterously beautiful head. She wanted that head in her lap beneath a tree somewhere, her fingers in its hair, a picnic recently eaten and love all yet to be made.

It was hard to dissuade herself of the conviction that he was breathing. The more she tried to hold herself still, the less it seemed he was made of stone, but was in fact a living, gorgeous thing. She realized she'd been holding a hand over her mouth.

Sculpture is by and large a practice of the site-specific, Tristan had told her once. All sculptors factor in the presumed distance from the viewer. In looking at a sculpture, there is a collaboration between the viewer, the work, and the intervening air, so that flaws in the design can transmute, can convey the impression of perfection. Such had been the intention with this *David*. Tristan had not seen this *David*, though they had spoken of it. A sideways way of alluding to a time when they might see it together – or so she thought, at the time.

Distance can be a most forgiving medium. She felt some petal of her sadness and her solitude fall away.

15

2019

FIRE BROKE OUT in the roof of Notre-Dame Cathedral in Paris. It was April of his grandmother's first year in the home.

Adrian was chopping an onion when the news came through. His laptop was in the next room, where the wifi connection was, and he was watching the football. Now and again he checked Twitter. He refreshed his home feed and there it was: a smudge of smoke appearing out of the top of the cathedral. He wiped his hands over the apron and went back to the onion. The next time he refreshed the page, some twenty minutes later, the main video was one shot from the Île Saint-Louis, of the spire snapping and falling into a haystack of flame. He gasped, a huge, melodramatic gasp at the same moment the crowd in the video cried out; a woman could be heard screaming, *Non!*. He took the onions off the heat then, and sat on the sofa, scrolling. Darkness fell and videos appeared of crowds gathered on the streets around the Île de la Cité. Some sang 'Ave Maria' and got down on their knees to pray. He was struck by how many young people were singing, and that they knew the words. Later, there were the clips of other churches in Paris ringing their bells in solidarity, and then churches all across France were doing the same. He'd drunk half a bottle of wine by this point, and surprised himself by being in tears. The village church across the street from where he sat joined in, the depth of its peals from across the street harmonizing strangely with the tinny bells coming through his laptop speakers.

The next day he walked to the tabac and bought a copy of the newspaper, where the image ran over the fold. People were talking about it as they queued to buy bread.

He cycled to town and arrived shortly before lunch. His grandmother was in her wheelchair in the dining room, staring at her empty plate. He wheeled her into her room, the paper tucked under his arm. When he had positioned her away from the window, he gave it to her, saying loudly – Look, Nana, what happened yesterday. She didn't make a move to take it from him, so he unfolded it and smoothed it over her lap. – Nana. She looked at him vacantly, her eyes huge. He picked up her hand and placed it on the masthead, running her finger over the crenellated top edge, then remembered that she had little sensation in her fingers, so he moved her knuckle down onto it instead. At this she stirred, and turned her head very slowly to her lap. She was perfectly still for a moment, and then sucked in her breath. It rattled through her throat phlegmily. He squatted awkwardly by her side.

– How can this be? she said. She turned to look at him searchingly.

– And what of the windows?

– The windows?

– What has happened to the rose windows? She had grabbed his wrist, where it rested on the wheel of her chair. Her grip moved his tendons up against the bone. – The ones from the thirteenth century? The work of Jean de Chelles and Pierre de Montreuil. The largest rose windows in Europe.

Her eyes moved, wildly, over his face.

He remembered now that he had seen in one video that some of the windows on the sides of the cathedral no longer had glass in them.

– You'll have to read this and tell me, Nana, he said.

She released his wrist and brought her hand up to her face, over her eyes, and began to cry. The sound of her sobs lagged, then rasped out of her drily. She was shaking. Snot began to run from her nostrils straight into her mouth and she did nothing to stop it. Embarrassed, he got up and went into her bathroom to look for tissues. While he was in there, he saw that the towel rack had been ripped from the wall, and now dangled by a single loose screw. When he handed her the tissue, she took it but did nothing with it, instead crumpling it in her hand, held at her temple. He took it from her again and dabbed at her face. He tried to tell her to blow her nose and gave her back some soft slaps. He didn't know what to do and she didn't show any signs of stopping. He tried to talk to her but she didn't seem to hear him. He considered just backing out of the room without saying goodbye. In the end he sat there, trying to think of other things, until it wound down of its accord. It would soon be time for her lunch.

Already there was talk of the cathedral's restoration. The president had called it the national destiny. Adrian pondered this idea and found it suspect.

– What will they do? She was looking up at him. – Will they make it as it was before, or will they make it anew, fireproof?

– I'm not sure, Nana.

– They must not make it fireproof. It is not as the master masons would have wanted it. They must use—

Here her talk broke off, he felt her searching for a word or a phrase but he was unable to help. He watched her reaching for it.

– They must use . . . *les matériaux nobles*. Stone and oak. They thought the stone was a living thing, you see. It sang for them.

– What do you mean, Nana? Who?

– The stone sings. It's how they tested for flaws. You hit it and you listen. It is what some of the master masons said. That they could hear it singing, that it sang for them. All across Europe, in the time of cathedral-building. We know quite a lot about the people who built them. Each mason had his mark. You were paid per finished stone. They kept ledgers. Do you see?

– Why do you know so much about it?

She looked up at him flatly.

– Men I loved once. Her gaze flicked to the corner of the ceiling, then sidelong at him. He sensed her changing tack abruptly. – We took you. Your mother and I. You went very serious and said you knew why they were called the medieval times. You said 'it was the middle of the evil times'.

A carer, a beautiful, witty woman named Samia, knocked loudly and put her head round the door. – *C'est l'heure du déjeuner!* Adrian smiled and nodded. His grandmother hadn't seen or heard.

– It's time for your lunch, Nana.

She nodded slowly in resignation. He wheeled her out into the dining room, where the carers moved about the tables, laying up the starter: some kind of pureed remoulade.

She kept the newspaper clutched in her lap, and as he left he heard her asking the other residents about it insistently, saying, *Regardez-ça!*

The next time Adrian visited, he would try to reprise this conversation, only to find that she did not know what he was talking about. It had slid out of her permanently, like shingle.

16

1961

WHEN MARGARET RETURNED to Rome for the autumn term, it was a fevered city. The Council was coming.

Rumours surrounding a Second Vatican Council had blown through the city for a time, like flame. It had been announced in 1959, to the great surprise of many. There had been talk of the pope summoning bishops, over two thousand of them, but also representatives of other churches – the Coptics, the Greek and Russian Orthodox – to discuss how to modernize the Church for a new millennium. It was to be the greatest gathering of global Christianity the world had ever seen, and the most ambitious examination of its doctrine since the Reformation.

The history of the Church had been punctuated by these councils, of course, but at intervals of several centuries, and their outcomes tended to be quite concentrated on a single issue: there had been the problem of icon-worship at The Second Council of Nicaea in 787, clerical celibacy at the First and Second Lateran Councils in 1123 and 1139; the reactionary, Counter-Reformation doubling-down at the Council of Trent, 1545–63, and the First Vatican Council's contribution of papal infallibility in 1869–70.

All of the above Margaret could strike from her fingertips like other information of its ilk: the Tudor monarchs, consequential inventions of the Industrial Revolution, names of the conquistadors, Russian novelists. She could go deeper into them and their ramifications – she had received high marks in the essays in which she did so – but this new Council meant watching the debates balloon and dilate in all their intricate and sometimes dead-end detail. She wanted to track each question through the papers, go for coffee with her lecturers and quiz them, stay up late talking it over with the sisters.

The First Vatican Council had concluded almost a century before by condemning the spirit of its times: socialism, liberalism, secularism, modernism, rationalism. Between the Council of Trent and the First Vatican Council, there had been three hundred years, an Enlightenment; the very concept of the individual human self had been redrawn. And between the First and the now Second Vatican Council, the change was only accelerating. Margaret felt the rush of it all in the balls of her feet; it flickered in her peripheral vision. Women had moved in that century, across from the jurisdiction of chattel law to that of the person. They had suffrage now, polio vaccination programmes, the lubricated condom, the H-bomb. The great mass of the Church was lumbering out of a deep and dark frankincensy fug in order to meet a new century. The word being used was *aggiornamento*: *mise à jour*. A bringing up to date.

Margaret and her peers were running over with optimism, with hope. It felt so enlivened. It was lit with the great questions of contraception, abortion, opening up the clergy, priestly celibacy, freedom of theological research, overpopulation, what marriage and family were *for*.

These were all, Margaret knew, questions about women. What women were for.

Now that the Council was in fact beginning, the city was thronged with journalists. They filled the bars within a two-mile radius, speaking in imperial languages, smoking, gesticulating grandly.

Margaret slept with one, an American, in the hard bed of his pensione. They had had an animated conversation about the ecumenical movement, Margaret matching him drink for drink. We have so much to learn from the East, he kept saying. The sounds he made during sex amused her, but still she felt her body waking once more to the motions. It felt good. She found, to her intense relief, that her body did indeed remember. All the marble nuns of Rome sat up and howled for her pleasure.

She woke in his bed in the grey light, her naked back sticking slightly to the wall. She left quietly and climbed the Aventine Hill to Santa Sabina, stopping by the terrace of the Aranci. Smog over St Peter's. She could smell the oranges as she came up the hill. There was oregano growing out of cracks in the walls. Dawn and brake dust were beginning to stir over the circolare.

The view was like the first sip of a much-anticipated white wine, cold and lucent, flinging its own light wantonly against the walls. Wine which woke and warmed the mouth even as it cooled it. She sat there for perhaps an hour. She was reading and making notes on the Gospels of Matthew and Luke. Beneath her clothes, her body hummed, awake again.

She crossed the Tiber and looked to St Peter's, where at that moment, men of another century were speaking about sex and love. The Patriarch of Antioch and All the East was taking his turn at the microphone (countered by Cardinal Ottaviani, Cardinal Tisserant, Cardinal Bea), saying: 'Marriage should not be split into the primary aim of procreation, with loving companionship a mere secondary consideration. Should we not ask if some attitudes are outmoded and, perhaps, the result of a kind of bachelor psychosis?'

Back in her room at the college, she washed her diaphragm and replaced it in its box. She clicked the bivalve of it shut.

One Wednesday, she was in the laundry (she went less and less these days, as her confidence in her own Italian grew), working with the young woman whose sheets they'd helped to wash the year before, prior to her wedding. Her name was Rezia. They were rinsing white cotton shirts in very hot water. Margaret looked up from the basin to see Rezia suddenly green-gilled. Before Margaret could help her to a chair, she had heaved forward and vomited into the water. She looked up at Margaret horrified, apologetic.

– *Nostro lavoro!* she cried. *Mi dispiace molto!*

Already, Giulia, Rezia's mother, was running over bearing a cloth and a cup of water. Someone else was bringing her a chair. The work of the room stilled, and the women gathered round.

She was pregnant of course.

She began to cry violently. She was saying that it was too early. *Abbiamo preso precauzioni*, she was saying. We were so careful. Giulia stroked her daughter's hair and nodded, but Beatrice, who was older, said gravely – Do not say that. *Stato benedetta*. Blessed.

Beatrice's son had been killed in Ethiopia when he was twenty years old.

– But not yet! Rezia said. Her hands were chapped and shaking. Even as Beatrice shook her head, she withdrew from her apron a flat dented tin of salve, and began to dab it onto the backs of Rezia's knuckles.

– Give thanks, came a caustic voice from outside the immediate circle of women, that you are *già sposata*. Already married.

It was Aurora, whose task it was to wash the sanitary pads, precisely because she had got pregnant, while still living in her father's house.

– *Ma mamma*, said Rezia, her eyes reaching for her mother's face, *ho paura*.

I am afraid.

Margaret moved to change the water in the basin and start afresh on the wash. Bile swirled in it like smoke.

– Let us hope, said Giulia, for this pill they speak of. I hope we can have it soon.

All the women Margaret knew were talking about it.

– No, said Beatrice in a disappointed voice. Rezia looked from her to her mother, smoothing the tears off over her cheeks.

– We shall have to see, Margaret said, if it is approved

here. And what the Council says about it. They will make a pronouncement.

The women's heads turned to her and they nodded solemnly.

– Let us hope, said Giulia, and with that the bell rang for their lunch hour.

17

2019

When he went to visit his grandmother she asked him, 'What game are you playing? You've got them all wrapped around your little finger, haven't you?' She didn't know what time it was and wouldn't believe him. 'That's what you say,' holding a piece of bread like irrefutable proof. 'This is what they give the prisoners here.' Leaning forward over her daily carafe of red wine. 'We're on a ship. All these people, all these other people' – swinging her arm ineffectually round the room – 'are *dead.*'

Another time she told him how, had things been different, she would have liked to have been an alpaca farmer. He had to deduce that they were alpacas – she kept saying, 'They were very attractive, these animals. Quite fluffy. The fluff once harvested is very good for knitting.'

They thought it had been caused by a stroke, but one insufficiently significant to show up on a brain scan. A ghost gathering its hems through the mind.

She has stopped brushing her teeth, such that they are grouted in something thick, yellowed, and a bit creamy-looking.

Every three weeks or so, he trims her fingernails, which

grow quickly, and chip in a way which looks painful, and gather brown filth under them. He forces himself not to think about what this could be, as she has most things done for her these days, and is no longer going outside. When he trims her fingernails, he pulls her in her wheelchair right up to the armchair, so their knees are touching. Then he places her hands on an old piece of newspaper. He takes each hand in turn and clips the nails with scissors.

It is a good way of being gentle with her, of making sure she is touched. And it means that he is close enough, and taking up enough of her field of vision, to be able to talk to her without shouting. When his grandmother's hands are in his lap like this, he is stunned every time by their beauty. They are long, the fingers increasingly curved by arthritis; they remind him of an early-medieval sculpture.

He lifts each hand in turn, holding it almost in greeting, halfway between a courtly kiss and a handshake. He concentrates hard, not wanting to catch the cuticles. After, he goes back over them with a nail file. Again, he wonders and worries that this might be uncomfortable for her, but she keeps her same soft smile and makes small noises of pleasure in her throat, and she looks him in the eye, and occasionally she winks at him. Then he folds the newspaper in half and takes it into the bathroom and tips the clippings into the toilet bowl. He spends a few minutes rubbing moisturizer into his grandmother's hands. He repeats the process with her feet.

Cherry season comes and goes. Adrian brings a big bag to her, and sits working out their stones with a butter knife. The whole time she is asleep, her head lolling forward onto her chest. The carers try to wake her, calling her name into her good ear, stroking her hair insistently. She opens her eyes wanly, unseeingly, then closes them again. – *Regardez, Madame Fletcher, c'est votre petit fils. Et il vous a amené des cerises*, they say: Look, it's your grandson, he's brought you cherries. But it doesn't work. She answers *Oui*, as if she is being called from somewhere very deep, but doesn't open her eyes. Eventually he leaves them by her plate. He gets back on his bike and coasts down the hill. Tears gather in the corners of his eyes.

His mother flies thousands of miles to sit on the end of his grandmother's bed, smooth her hand over the quilt, and say, too brightly, What have you been up to?

Then Nana launches into telling them about people she knew who'd gone to Switzerland 'to have their lives taken'.

He watches his mother writhe on the hook of it. In the laundry room afterwards, while his mother cries and says, I want her to die, he rubs her back.

– She wanted me to google it for her and I said you can't ask that of me.

– Well done, he says.

His grandmother thinks he is a carer; thinks he is her father; thinks he is Gung. Time is collapsing all around her. The paper calendar on the wall displays the wrong date for months. The swifts scream under the eaves where they nest. She requests a rosary and he digs out his grandfather's, which is enormous, and must have swung to his navel; and she thumbs it, looking out to an invisible elsewhere. The bells keep the hours, seven until ten. His bicycle ticks beneath him, back and forth.

– Eggs like planets, set adrift, one by one.
– What?
– There are many different kinds of time. You would do well to realize. Stone time. Star time. The quick and the dead.

He gets a job. Back in London. When he goes to explain it to her, she stares at him, then says: – There are some things you could do for me. I need more bread. And soap. And *apples*. At the bus stop on the morning he leaves, he weeps.

PART II

18

1963

Miss Bendelow, the new theology teacher, arrived on the penultimate day of August. News of her coming had sent the nuns down the corridors at speed, whispering with great emphasis, *she, she*. David was at home, frying the last of the courgette flowers (the vine had been prolific all summer long) – dipped in a light batter, pipetted with cottage cheese; ricotta was a laughable proposition in Britain – when the news came. Sister Catherine, one of the novices, came barrelling down the hill to the presbytery in her orthopaedic sandals and stood breathless in the open kitchen door.

– Father Fletcher, Father Fletcher! She's arrived, Father Fletcher!

– Good evening to you too, Sister Catherine. Have you had a look at her yet? He scooped up a stray drop of cheese with a finger.

– No, Father, Sisters Michael and Louise have gone to meet her at the station.

– Oh, so she's not actually arrived then yet, has she? What did you have to run down the hill to see me for? He smiled kindly at her, the smile he'd been trained to give when a mild intrusion on his privacy occurred in the off hours. Sister

Catherine had no answer. He gave her a glass of lemonade and offered her a flower fresh from the pan, pinched in the tongs. She must have been twenty-three or so, still girlishly greedy. She was puzzled by the flower, but declared it delicious, and walked back up the hill towards the college, licking the grease from her fingers.

Margaret's arrival at Rugby station felt like the beginning of a joke, or its punchline. Two nuns and a laywoman walk into a bar. No recognition between strangers could have been so easy: look for the women in the wimples. The woman who greeted Sisters Michael and Louise now was thirty-six. She was wearing her hair in a severe knot, a white shirt with a piecrust collar, a pinstriped brown pencil skirt and a jacket to match, like a man's blazer. It was the most demure outfit she could put together, having changed in a cramped toilet at Birmingham New Street from her trousers earlier on in the journey. It was to be the last concession she would make to their tastes. Her shoes were flat, unassuming Oxfords, which were the single most expensive thing she'd ever bought. She looked exhausted, and was, having caught the sleeper train from Rome to Paris the night before and woken for the first train to Calais.

The drive up to the college was full of anodyne pleasantries. She was caught unawares by how suddenly moved she was to be talking about the weather again. The nuns quizzed her amicably about her accent, competing with each other to situate it. The younger one had pale red eyebrows, and spoke with enthusiasm. She was as Margaret had hoped her new colleagues would be: young, invigorated, quick-witted and warm. And then the older sister mentioned a Father Fletcher, 'whom you will be working with', and Margaret's cheerful ease snagged.

– I beg your pardon?

– Father Fletcher. Our parish priest. Did no one tell you? The younger, driving nun was abruptly blushing, and she removed her hands from the steering wheel one by one to wipe them on her thighs.

Margaret assured her that no one had.

– Well. That was an unfortunate oversight. You will be sharing your teaching duties with Father Fletcher.

To supervise her, she imagined. Rein her in. She could imagine that had been the instruction from on high. Some careerist bishop speaking chap to chap. She conjured an image of him, this imminent colleague: old, his nose mycelial with burst blood vessels no doubt. Dandruff. The prospects of the job laid out before her curdled quickly. Teaching under the thumb of a priest hadn't figured in her vision. She had wanted women, their company, their minds running free when there were no men around. Her throat tightened. Here it was: the point of the priesthood. In the same way that newspapers had stringers in Fez or the secret services had their man in Havana or Istanbul or Beirut: the Church posts a man to every town, burgh and village, tells him what to say to the people who live there. Makes him their secret-keeper. She knew well how the debates about female clergy were going in Rome. Women, it was said by several cardinals at the ongoing Council, had not the wherewithal for sublimation; they were too much of the body and of the world. It's true, she *was* of the world. She saw it as no weakness. Yes. She would figure out this priest, and make sure he left her and her teaching well alone. They were teaching in a women's college. She was a woman, therefore would have a rapport with the students which he could not. There was little, regardless of any Rome-imposed hierarchy, which could be done about that.

The buildings of the college, as they came up the drive, were classic mid-to-late-nineteenth-century Puginism on the cheap: brick in black, red and the occasional grubby London yellow, with cramped Gothic arches. The windows were mostly unadorned, and paned in squares with the thick watery colour of bottle bottoms. Her room was at the end of a corridor of sisters' quarters. It was tiny, little more than a storage cupboard, she thought, and had most likely served as one until very recently. It smelled of dust recently disturbed and cleared. It held one cot bed, narrow and made up with a faded blue wool blanket. Above it hung a small crucifix, made of porcelain, and on the adjoining wall, a print of the Virgin in a star-spangled cloak of baby blue. Over the bedside table was a slim slice of window, the glass warped and distorting, but some panes clear enough to see the grounds rolling out below: a sloping open lawn and at its edge, a line of enormous cedar trees. Under them, a link of benches. In the foreground, right below the window, was a walled kitchen garden. Fruit trees were pinned to its bricks at the outer edges, and raised beds were frilled with heads of lettuce. Herbs filled neat tight borders and a file of raspberry or pea plants were kept in check by a triangulation of canes. A nun was digging with gusto for turnips, straightening up at periods to shake the dirt off them with large swings of her arms. Margaret felt a swell of affection for this place already, the deep architectural nostalgia of England. She began to unpack.

❧

She didn't meet her colleague the priest until she'd been there two days. She sat on a bench against the garden wall, catching the last of the sun. He strode up the hill like a lighter of beacons. He wore his cassock and the shape of it opened and closed as he walked. As he came closer, she saw that he held a pair of glasses in one hand, and the little finger of his right bore a signet ring.

He was shockingly, startlingly handsome. He was, she guessed, about forty.

– Miss Bendelow.

He did not speak loudly, he was at a distance of twelve paces from her or more, but his voice travelled like that of an actor. She wondered briefly if they trained you for that: the acoustics of mildewed stone. She smiled at him. – You must be Father Fletcher.

– The one and only! He gathered a fistful of cassock in either hand and gave a mock-curtsey. They both laughed. They shook hands. His had small calluses and she wondered what from.

– I am sorry I have only been able to come now, when you've already been here a while. Thursdays I go to St Benedict's Hospital and see to the dying.

– Oh?

– I like it very much actually.

– Ah yes.

– So you have just come from Rome?

– Yes, I got the train straight up. Almost in one shot.

– And what did you miss most while you were away?

– You know, it's funny. I hadn't really thought about it but you're the first to ask. Pickled things, I think.

He laughed, a real laugh that came out of him like bubbles from deep water.
– Really!
He was congenial, peppering her with questions and asking all the polite sort of things: how was her journey and was she settling in well, but there was a wariness which lurked behind the eyes.
– How long have you been a priest?
– Ten years.
– And this parish all that time?
– Yes, I've been very lucky.
– And you were in Rome too?
– Yes, forty-six to fifty-three.
– I imagine it is very different now.
A portcullis slotted into place behind his eyes with his perfunctory, teeth-bared – Quite. The bell rang for supper and she stood up quickly. She motioned hesitantly over her shoulder. – Will you be joining us?
– No, Miss Bendelow, I shall leave you to it. It is my lot to eat alone.
She couldn't tell if it was a joke, but he had turned away and was walking quickly. – I will see you in action on Monday! he called out over his shoulder. Good evening!

She, though, saw him in action first, that Sunday. She filed into the church deliberately late so that she could sit at the back, apart.
He wore vestments embroidered with crimson and violet leaping fish. His voice was sonorous and slow. His singing of the psalms had that learned strangeness absolved of

time. The chalice was perfectly proportioned against his hands.

It was an intimate thing, this one-man show before an audience of a hundred or so, but the performer was both there and not there. He seemed to be out of his body in some way. It wasn't boredom, or overuse. His movements weren't rote, so much as exhibiting some deeper state of consciousness. He gave himself wholly to the rites demanded of him; he gave so little of himself to his audience.

Monday's lesson – her first – arrived, and the idea was for him to sit in and observe. He took up a seat at the back of the classroom with a notepad. The students filed in, all young women with glossy hair, wearing nondescript clothes. This class was, traditionally, a rote prerequisite for these women, to make them eligible for employment in Catholic schools and so they could teach the catechism to primary school children. Margaret took a poor view of this: it was formulaic, unimaginative teaching which would only make formulaic, unimaginative teachers. Unbeknownst to her, as of yet, was that David agreed with her. What Margaret hoped to achieve was ambitious: proper, rigorous theology in order to turn out, as David liked to repeat in his mind – he was mulling its usefulness in a talk or possibly an article; he heard that the editors at *The Tablet* were quite open to more progressive opinion pieces these days – 'conscientious Catholics, not cabbages'.

When the bell rang to mark the lesson's beginning and the new teacher still was not there, the girls shifted slightly in their seats, unsure of what to do. Then she did come, entering with a bang of the door on its hinges, carrying an armload of books as she might an enormous sheaf of wheat. Her hair was up in a bun, wisping down from her crown to the spaces around her temples and her ears. As she entered, the students all rose to their feet. At this Miss Bendelow stopped, and a look of alarm blotted her face. – Oh ladies, you don't need to do that for me! In fact, I insist you do not. She deposited the books on the desk. – I am Miss Bendelow, but you may call me Margaret. There was a ripple through the room. She wrote it on the board for good measure. There was that pleasurable sound of the chalk coming into contact with the board for the first time. It was a beginning of something. David felt it announcing itself. Now the two words stood white and stark on the green, the colours of the Seven Sisters seen from the homegoing ferry: Margaret Bendelow.

– I am here to teach you theology. You do not know how lucky you are. You are young women and your predecessors of not so long ago would have been equipped with only prayers and the saints. Together, we have the opportunity to study moral theology, dogmatics and the liturgy! She grinned but the full effect seemed to be lost on the young women. – I look forward to getting to know you all (she was positively shining now), as I have just come from Rome and let me tell you, ladies, there is a revolution afoot. She raised her hands in the manner of someone drawing something out. Did she think she was a preacher? – You may have noticed that I am a woman and am wearing neither a wimple nor one of those. She flurried her fingers over her neck and simultaneously pointed with her chin towards the back of the room. Twenty bodies turned in twenty seats to look at David and the collar at his throat.

– I am only the third such group of women who have been able to even qualify for this line of work.

She was proud of it.

– Father Fletcher and I will be meeting over the next few days to plan and discuss the shape of the term for all of you, but the aim is to turn you out as thinking Catholics by the end of it.

David and Margaret worked together in the common room, preparing a loose curriculum for the coming weeks. Margaret wanted to assign their students Thomas Aquinas and St Augustine, but he disagreed. She was too ambitious, he said, and there was no need. She objected; she probed how he had reached this conclusion. He felt her feeling along the walls of his thinking, searching for cracks, and he recoiled. It had been a long time since his view on a matter had been challenged. When she sensed this, she changed tack, instead making what she hoped were enticing, though safe, suggestions. Let's start them off with some Boethius, she would say, or how about some Hildegard von Bingen? She coupled this approach with a continued stealth offensive on his rationale. Why did he want to whittle their teaching down to the bare, bereft essentials? Why had they hired her, if not for the new wave which she represented? She wanted him to admit it: that he didn't believe women should be taught to this level, that he was guardian to a millennia-old monopoly. She wanted also for him to realize that he was King Cnut against the tide.

But Margaret was wrong. He wanted to minimize the students' assigned reading because he feared it would be too dry for them; he didn't want to put them off with the looping multi-clause epistemology of the Middle Ages, where star-spotted leopards padded into the same pages of the monastic annals as a bout of clerical malady. He wanted to see it all made compelling and animate by sermonizing, and extemporizing wittily. This was, of course, the mode that *he* had been trained and primed for, and where he was most comfortable. He was fascinated, genuinely in awe, in fact, of how interesting she seemed to find the long slog of fourteenth-century mysticism. He knew it was a necessary stepping stone, but he couldn't quite understand her love, the dawn that bloomed on her face when she spoke of it. What she had, and what he gradually understood himself to lack, was a mature, intellectual grasp of the arc of it all. He had been born into Catholicism; it was in him like marrow, he had drawn it up, into all the coursing paths of his self: he had been entirely passive. It could never be rooted out. But she had converted – when feeling lost in life, and recently bereaved, but as an adult nonetheless. A more cynical man might have thought her conversion was a fad, and she a woman who followed fashions, but he could see that she was no such thing. Really, they would joke long afterwards, it would have been so much easier if that had been the case.

The problem was always that she was so singular. Belonging to no archetype. He felt ill-equipped to either apprehend or comprehend her.

They sparred at first. On the maleness of the priesthood. He said what he had been trained to say.
– Because the Apostles were men.
– But the Apostles were also Jews.

He remembered this way of talking, or one like it – adversarial, without allegiance – from his school days, but he had left it behind during his time at the seminary. It wouldn't be needed, because these matters were only to be discussed with your fellow seminarians, who would – should – be in agreement with you anyway.

But Margaret was different. What he had thought was an emulation of the male mode of conversation, which he knew was being deployed this very moment across the bright green benches of the Commons, or in the courts of law, was in fact a sharp, unguarded curiosity. She wanted to know how he arrived at his conclusions, how his thoughts were made.

Still, she had a coldness to her. Towards him. He couldn't blame her. He decided to be that which she did not expect.

He wore her down with strange questions and a wry exuberance. They walked the grounds together, under the windows, where they could always be seen.

– I had an unusual white wine once. It was delicious.

– Oh?

– It came from a vineyard on the coast of Sicily. A sandy vineyard, steep, looking over the sea.

You could smell it; you could feel the brush of the Mediterranean breeze on the end of your nose when you put it into the glass. A quiet terrace near the Appia Antica. An August afternoon, its promise purpling over him. Summer pleasures in a sunny city. The clear Tiber and its fronded dancing weeds. He remembered the first time he had seen it. For all its stature in the mind and history: it was small.

At other times he was seized by a whimsy which she liked. They helped to weed the kitchen garden, kneeling in the dirt side by side while junior sisters dug holes or assembled trellises in the far corners.

– What is your favourite stone fruit?
– Cherries.
– Ah, excellent choice.

She said the cherry season was always too short for her.

He laughed when she told him that when she'd visited the Sistine Chapel, it hurt her neck so much – looking up – she thought they ought to allow batches of people in on a timed basis, and that the room be filled with ranks of sun loungers, so you could lie on your back for twenty minutes and look at as much of the ceiling as you liked.

She had always been suspicious of good-looking men. He, however, had a guilelessness. A reluctance to concede he was gorgeous, an embarrassment that he didn't know what to do about it.

She remembered the long-ago admonition from her mother that, when dressing, one should show off one thing at a time: the legs, the shoulders, the back, the arms, the décolletage. The body was to be divided into assets which must be deployed with restraint. The nuns lived an extreme version of it; only their hands and the pale moons of their faces showing. She never saw their wrists or ankles; she didn't know what kind of hair they had. She knew what kind David had, his head a thing she could observe in the round, the light shining through his ears.

She registered at the local GP surgery and asked for the Pill. In Italy there had been only faint black-market whisperings by the time she left. Here she could have it. She ignored the doctor's glance at her left hand. Back at the college, she entered the communal bathroom on her corridor, opened the packet, silverfoil-carbuncled like a reliquary, and pushed out one of the egg-smooth white pills. The foil made a cracking noise as it gave way. The pill lay in the palm of her hand, getting sticky, as she looked for a glass and then water to fill it. As she tipped her head back to chase it down, she could feel its sugarshell dissolving as it passed over her tongue. She imagined it descending in the dark and sending its freedoms fizzing out into her blood. She could do any number of things now: meet friends or someone she might sleep with, walk the streets, eat at restaurants, and all the while it would be doing its invisible work in the walls of her. The plastic compact she kept them in was baby blue. She snapped it shut.

She had come loping out of the landscape with the horizon of his life looped up in her arms like washing line, and had lain it at his feet like guide rope. She blew in on a fresh breeze, carrying her armfuls of books. A medievalist. She wore bright colours: day coats with three-quarter sleeves in bright linen, skirts hemmed at the knee and sometimes shorter, big bell sleeves and empire waists, and sometimes flashes of her bare ankle at the tapering cuff of her trousers. What drew his eye the most was her hair, a great rush of it standing out among the wimples; strawberry blonde and always in complicated buns atop her head, swept up from her neck, where the small hollow between the tendons of her neck looked downy and soft. It passed underneath his nose, trailing a smell of trade winds, of spices. He caught himself wondering once what it would be like to put his fingers in its mass of curls. He pictured her putting the pins in one by one. Her mouth full of them, her concentration. The ache in her arms as she held them both above her head for so long.

The common room was beautiful, with a cornice and faded, thick-piled rugs. The windows had hinged inside shutters, painted cream, and there were fitted bookshelves – this was also the nuns' lending library, and was stocked with a joyous medley of books: from Graham Greene to Evelyn Waugh, and well-thumbed editions of Julian of Norwich or *The Consolations of Philosophy*. David and Margaret worked here in the evenings, when the others had left at the end of the day, going over lesson plans for the remainder of the week, marking papers. They listened to the radio and drank tea. The room was cold one evening, nearing November. It could only be heated by the fireplace under its moulded plaster mantelpiece. Margaret remembered her parents carefully portioning out their wood stack each winter. She pulled her cardigan closer round her shoulders.

– Are you hungry? David asked.

She was. They had just shaken the biscuit tin dry of shortbread fingers, and felt guilty.

– I have the remnants of a chicken back at the bungalow if you'd like.

She swallowed carefully.

– All right.

It was dark and they each took their briefcases under an arm and made their way down the hill by the light of the lamps which dotted the drive at long intervals.

Concentrating. A side effect of this being total silence. At one point she thought she stepped on a slug. Her heel slid and she almost lost her balance.

His house was new, tastefully built out of redbrick with huge plate glass windows which took up one whole side of the building. A lamp had been left on and from outside she could make out a living room with its familiar coordinates of sofa and armchair. The frames of prints glinted gold on the walls.

Inside he retrieved plates from a high cupboard. He bent down into the fridge and brought out a half-denuded chicken carcass on a blue and white dish. There was a bowl of green beans and roast potatoes. He turned away from her and began slicing the cold potatoes very thinly, rocking the knife deftly on the board.

He is a man making salad. This little labour. In his kitchen, at night. She feels they are in a painting by Edward Hopper: a cold square of glass, the way it runs with light like melting butter; and them the figures inside it, relations to one another as yet unknown.

– Do you drink beer? There are bottles in there. He motioned to the fridge.

She didn't know whether she drank beer. She'd never committed herself to finding out. She retrieved two bottles and opened them with the bottle opener affixed to a nearby wall. He put out his hand for one. They clinked; a pleasant, thick sound. The beer gave her a laconic, masculine feeling, as if she were one of the cricket players she had watched on the green growing up. The end of the day, among men, her body healthy and pleasantly tired. Stretched out on a grassy bank, the summer waters sauntering past.

He was making a vinaigrette now, mixing mustard with red cider vinegar, tossing the beans and sliced potatoes in it. – Would you like some bread? She would. He pivoted round from the counter he'd been turned to as if he were dancing and put the dishes down in front of her at the table. He picked up a long loaf of bread and held it out to her. She took one end of it and he didn't let go. She pulled and felt him pulling. The bread came apart into two chunks. He smiled at her. She observed him, sipping her beer, feeling again like a man in a bar with the prerogatives of observation. He was so neat in his movements. This was his kitchen and he was working in it. He was a man who could carve a chicken and knew what to do with limp leftover beans. He lived alone. She knew he had a housekeeper but she was not in evidence. Perhaps she had roasted the chicken, originally. She could not recall ever having had a meal prepared for her by a man other than her father.

They ate standing up, leaning against opposite counters, using only their forks. To sit down across from one another at a table would have been too much. Right now she was his colleague; she had missed supper, she was hungry and he had given her something to eat. This was his role: to give sustenance of one kind or another. He smiled at her. She, feeling bold, swilled beer round her mouth. Then they graded papers until nine. She walked back in the dark. There was the smell of cedar roses underfoot as she crunched over them.

After that they agreed it was probably best if they worked henceforth at his house. It was foolish, they agreed, to be burning through so much wood to heat the common room – it was inefficient anyway, they added – and this way they didn't need to stop their work to eat. They could eat together, at his house, and just carry on until the day's work was done. Margaret informed Sister Augusta on a Tuesday morning, putting her head round her office door to deliver the news. Sister Augusta said – I see. And her mouth went small and tight. – Please make sure you are back before nine so someone can let you in, Miss Bendelow.

19

An evening in December's damp chill. The colours drab and wintered, the land dormant. They had done this enough times now that she took the lead making tea, lifting the kettle to the hob, fetching down the pot. They moved around one another in a grooved way. He leant against the counter with a heavy sigh, and unfastened his Roman collar. It came away with a starched, clothy pop and lay in his hands looking like a rib. She raised her eyebrows at him.

– They called these taxi lights at the seminary. They told us never to run for the bus when we were wearing them.

– Oh yes?

– It makes people panic to see a priest run.

Her laughter like a yearned-for storm.

There was a slight line on his neck above where it had been. Grime, or the sun. He kept the black shirt buttoned up to the top. She caught herself wondering what kind of body lay beneath. Did he have dimples in his back? What pattern of hair on his chest? All these parts of his body which went about the world unseen. The kettle's interrupting scream.

– Where does the term 'dog collar' come from? she asked. Do you think it is an anti-Catholic insult?

– Most certainly.
– And you, do you like the lead?

He flinched. At times like these she frightened him. They could talk for hours, their conversations running freely and easily. But then it hit him like a pane: that she had given almost nothing up for her command of things, whereas he had. But she had paid for none of it. The skin of experience glimmered over her like fur, she slunk in it and sometimes seemed to taunt him with it.

– What was it like? To be called.

He stilled, pushed air out from between his lips. He played with small things at the edge of his vision. His ring. The buckle of his watch. The buttons at his cuff.

– I think you have felt it too. Just perhaps for something else.

– What do you mean?

– The way you talk about certain things. You have a look.

– A look?

When she spoke of poems, paintings, pockets of time and their consequence – her soul seemed to leap into her face. She became so consummately animate, so *there*, close beneath her skin.

– When I talk about what? she said.

– You know.

– No, I don't. Tell me.

– Art. Raphael. Mannerism. The Sienese School. You know.

– Go on.

– Milton. You are so unashamed.

He meant in her intelligence. He'd never known another like her. Of course he could appreciate how it could be seen as arrogance, but what he saw was an innocence, a love which was unabashed and undeterred. What had she been given in greater measure, to have this joy and wit course through her planed face, as she spoke to him of Marvell, *Macbeth*, of a gynaecological treatise from the fifteenth century and its link to the Crucifixion?

She nodded, very slowly.

– By the way. I can't do this time next week. I have a Christmas party to go to.

– You must go to many, she said, smiling.

– This one is the archbishop's.

20

Archbishop Dwyer's house was overly large, a brash mock-Tudor frontage on a wide street which should have been planted with more trees. The trunk of a wisteria wound its way through the fence like an anaconda. Desultory paper chains hung in the windows and on the banister of the wide dark staircase. A drinks table was set up in the hall, ranked with glasses of sherry. Everywhere, men in black clustered, talking chummily.

This was one of the two annual opportunities for all the clergy of the archdiocese to see one another. The other was Dwyer's summer party, held outside in the garden at the back, where there was an expansive lawn and borders deep with flowering shrubs. David had always enjoyed these occasions; had relished slipping back into collegiate habits of talk, observing the liquid elegance with which the younger priests could slide past the objectionable views of the older; and as the evening wore on, hands clapping emphatically on backs, the sherry loosening them and giving way to the contents of hip flasks, passed back and forth on the stairs.

Now, Christmas 1963, David noticed small groups of his

colleagues, close to him in age, standing in corners with their backs turned to the rest of the room, their jaws moving urgently and angrily over their talk. He walked up to one group. They fell silent and gave him a weighing look.

– Fletcher. How are you? We hear you're working with the new laywoman over at St Genevieve's. How's that going? He saw the contemptuous smiles on some of the group, but Mack, who was the priest at St Joan of Arc's in Stoke, and who'd asked the question, was sincere.

– Well, I think. A tough nut to crack at first. I think I wasn't what she expected.

– What did she expect?

– Oh, you know.

David turned back into the room, gesturing with a gracious sweep of his gaze, at the groups of men stationed near the drinks tables, their fingers thick and purpled over the stems of their glasses, their jowls webbed with puce. Some were already gesticulating clumsily, and he heard one use that emotive word, *unborn*.

– We were just talking about the Council. The discussions about worker priests and a married clergy and so on. This was offered by Poole, a short, freckled man who was priest for Yoxall. He wore the thick-rimmed rectangular glasses which were currently in fashion. Given their uniform, there was little latitude for the priests to express any sense of, or allegiance to, modernity. But glasses were a possibility. If a man had fashionable glasses, you could hint at things, and see how he took them.

– We were agreeing, said Mack, speaking soft and low, that men can be the clergy for children because man has been a child, but women need a female clergy, and married people need a married clergy. Experience alone can equip us with the wisdom we need.

To be good shepherds, David thought, finishing the sentence in his head. It was what the rhythm dangled for. They often caught themselves speaking like this: the Bible's archaic inverted syntax worked its way into their normal speech, and they turned out sentences like it on the lathes of their minds. David glanced back over his shoulder. He could see Dwyer prowling with a bottle in his hand, offering top-ups, watching. One of the purple priests split into gluttonous laughter.

An older, stooped man named Wilson, with a hard knot of Adam's apple protruding over the bucktooth of his collar, appeared at David's elbow and said beakily to Mack:

– You won't get far with talk like that, my boy. Will you?

Mack made to speak, then closed his mouth. He looked down at the empty toothpick in his fingers and twirled it. Silence coagulated over the group.

– I think Mack means, said Poole, that the right sort of life experience might be useful in one's ministry.

David winced internally. It was a bold synopsis, and the older man was evidently not the type who would take it well.

– What sort of life experience could you possibly be alluding to? Wilson smiled with the sport of it.

– Well, ventured Mack, I for one struggle to advise members of my congregation on their marriages, not being married myself.

– You know as well as I do that we're above all that.

Mack stood up straighter. – With respect, he began.

Oh dear, thought David.

– In no other line of work would you be accorded respect

and expertise without first having had some kind of experience. It would be considered fraudulent.

Wilson's lower jaw loosened in affront. He had been drinking red wine. Dwyer was known for the quality of his cellar; David could see the coating of cabernet on his teeth.

– And what, pray tell, do you think our archbishop will make of that? Shall we ask him?

No sooner had Wilson turned around to look for him than Dwyer was moving across the foyer towards them: long-legged, vulpine.

– Hello, chaps. And how are we all?

– I was just hearing from this young man, Wilson began. Mack met Dwyer's gaze. He wasn't young. David guessed he was about five years younger than himself. Wilson continued: – He thinks the clergy should be able to marry. He feels *inexperienced*.

– Do you now? Dwyer's face was flat. And you think this is the forum? He made a lazy encompassing gesture.

Mack looked at the bottom of his empty glass.

– You'll find no more drink in my house if you keep talking like that.

David and the other men did as they had been trained to do since childhood. They stood and took it, silently.

– What was your name? Dwyer said calmly. When Mack answered, Dwyer nodded, then crossed the room whence he came, beckoning with a single finger to a small man David presumed to be his secretary. Together they disappeared through a dark wooden door. Wilson tipped his head back to drain his glass, then grinned. He rounded on David.

– You're the chap in Monks Kirby, aren't you? You're the one who is having to deal with that woman. David had heard *woman* pronounced that way before, as if it was a hard word, shit being scraped off a shoe.

– Miss Bendelow has a fine mind.

Wilson puffed out his chest. They were all, David could see now, giving him more than he'd hoped for this evening.

– She cannot possibly have the sobriety required to *penetrate* into the Church's mysteries. Those belong to us, he said, including them all with a sloshing half-moon of his glass. Us and us alone.

This is what David had always been taught, by default, by fiat. He had absorbed it unthinkingly, and only now did it strike him as grotesque. But: Margaret was not here to hear it, so he need not defend her. Instead he gave Wilson what he wanted: a defeated inclination of the head, and then he excused himself.

When he told her about it all later that week, she giggled. Then the sudden turn.

– And you? What do you think about married clergy? She did not break his gaze.

– Clerical celibacy is how we priests practise sublimation.

She turned the clean line of her jaw up towards him. He watched the thought gather on the edge of it, like a diver.

– You and I both know that's a doctrinal fig leaf.

– It is an ancient aspect of the priesthood.

– Not so ancient. Clerical celibacy only gets cemented at the Second Lateran, a mere eight hundred years ago. And even then, only as a means of countering corruption. Too many priests inheriting their churches from their fathers.

– Marriage is a distraction to the priest, who must give

himself fully to his congregation. Celibacy is a gift I have given.

– But how does it equip you for your work?

– You are thinking of that passage from Timothy, aren't you? 'But if a man knows not how to rule his own house, how shall he take care of the church of God?'

Here we go, he thought. We are crossing over into the matter of it. If we were overheard, it would be as dry as bone to some. To others, incendiary heresy. He felt both of these facts fighting it out in his chest.

– It's not really about a man managing his household, she continued. The rest of that passage is: 'The watcher must have an impeccable character. Husband of one wife.' Then it goes on to list the necessary qualities: he must be temperate, discreet, courteous, hospitable; a good teacher; not a heavy drinker, nor hot-tempered; gentle. *Then* it asks the question: his own house, church of God.

– 'Watcher'? Which translation is that?

– My own.

They let this fact pool between them for a moment.

– The word in the Septuagint, she adds, is *skeptomai*.

– What is that? Here was where his knowledge met hers. He had not studied the Septuagint to the same degree. Latin had been his language for the Church, in all things.

– Relating to inspect, respect, scope, spectacle, speculate. She takes a sip of her drink. – Spy.

He catches his breath and she sees him do it.

She has done what they must not do: gone back through the languages and unknotted them. He is suddenly, he realizes, afraid, even; just as he admires the Janus-faced elegance of what she has done.

– In the King James and Douay-Rheims it is translated as bishop. The Latin is *episcopatum*. In Hebrew it is overseer. Site manager. Boss. So on. Shepherd is of course the popular choice for the vernaculars.

Here is where her knowledge strides past his. She is hitting him with a precision he does not possess.

– So what is your point?

– Religion gives us the concept of daily life, and a way of handling its tediums, and marriage is one of its great means. Marriage is a mode of witness, an epistemology. To bar people from marriage is to prevent them from this way of knowing. And a means to maturity, too. Or at least, marriage should be all these things, and more.

At this last point he flinched.

– You hold nothing back, Miss Bendelow.

– Why should I, Father Fletcher?

– And for women?

– What about them?

– What is good in marriage, for women?

– Nothing, as of yet. She winked at him and went to light a cigarette, opening the window. – We must refashion what marriage can be.

Advent was a busy period for him. In his time in the archdiocese he had become friends with his counterparts in neighbouring parishes. In one of the picturesque neighbouring villages, he had struck up friendships with the Church of England vicars (interfaith rapprochement in action! they had joked), and, in partnership with the shops of the local high street, had started a tradition of Wednesday carolling in the month of December. Each Wednesday, the shops stayed open later. The pub sold mulled wine and a crowd from the surrounding area gathered. The stand-up piano from the church would be wheeled up and down the street, stopping at intervals for the carols. David drafted Mack in to play it, and he bashed at the keys with music hall enthusiasm. David's job was to conduct, for which he stood on a chair and shouted above the assembled people. The first Wednesday Margaret marvelled at how it was all allowed. Surely these were the sorts of antics which would be clamped down on once word reached the higher-ups. The Church of England should be left alone to these undignified outreach efforts. But quickly her fears fell away: David, when he got up onto the chair before the rosy-cheeked crowd, was self-assured in the silliness of it all. When he flourished his hands to move them through the songs, he grinned from ear to ear. He flicked his scarf over his shoulder with camp panache. It was, Margaret had to concede, profoundly appealing. Everyone rocked on the balls of their feet in time with the romp of 'Good King Wenceslas' and swayed for the solace of 'In the Bleak Midwinter'.

Afterwards they went to the pub all together. The other priests shook Margaret's hand enthusiastically and wanted to know what Rome during the early Council had been like. David, sat across the table in the booth, smiled confidingly at her. She noticed he was rubbing his red-tipped ears from the cold. The next week she gave him a hat she'd knitted. When he got up to conduct, the bobble of it danced in time with his movements.

She went to Sheffield for Christmas, stayed with Eileen and Carol. Watched the quiet way they moved around one another. She did not write to David, but she wanted to. She could think of no sufficient pretext. He was, she imagined, being kept busy, and had no time to think of her, whereas she, in the quiet of the year's last turning, found herself thinking of him too much.

She was not to know that he did think of her. He kept a quiet tally of things to tell her about when she returned. He stored them subtly about his person, such that he himself could not confess to their whereabouts or import. The news came quietly, after Epiphany, that Mack had been moved on to another parish, on the other side of the diocese. He hadn't been told explicitly why, but they all knew his comments at the Christmas party were the reason.

21

In February, Margaret wanted to take the students to see services in the churches of other denominations. She mentioned it to David. – That's beyond my pay grade, he replied. She started. She was still learning that he was part of a long chain of command. It hadn't occurred to her that she needed permission. – You'll have to write to the next man up and say why you want to do that, he said.

So she did. She spent an evening perfecting a letter to Dwyer, and showed it to David for his approval. He agreed that it was a winsome piece of rhetoric and he wished her the best with it. He knew how it would go, though.

The answer was no.

Now she was pacing the narrow corridor of carpet between his sofa and his coffee table. She made sudden, voluble gestures with her arms. Her drink slid over the rim of her glass and onto the floor. It was Campari (expensive, imported). It would be sticky later. Mrs Cooper would scrub at it hard on her hands and knees and wonder where it came from.

– How, Margaret was saying, are our students supposed to survive, and do the work that we are training them to do, in a pluralist England, if this is the attitude? She fell back into the sofa heavily, sighing. She reached her hand down her shin and rolled the ball of her ankle through the joint.

Her optimism was crashing into the nature of Catholic central command, mangling itself. – When this kind of thing happens, our students will conclude that the Church's leaders act out of fear. And this earns not their respect, make no mistake about it – her index finger loosened itself from her tumbler and pointed straight at him – but their contempt and suspicion.

He nodded. – I quite agree with you, you know.

She eyed him warily, then took in the room again. It was warmly furnished, not by a bachelor at all it seemed. There were rugs and cushions and shelves full of books. Who had helped him with that? She had lived almost exclusively in rooms. He had a house. Full of objects and no other people. Whereas she, she supposed, was an empty house, needing to be peopled. Or so it felt (so the advertisements screamed).

– Who did you talk with about these things, before me?

He shrugged. His answer was more earnest than intended.

– No one. There has only been you.

– What do you mean?

– I don't think I really thought of these things before you.

It was almost true. Before Margaret and before the Second Council, he had been content in his role. He liked the structure and the stricture of it, it was familiar to him. He liked presenting himself for the tasks demanded of him at the stipulated hours. With his colleagues, he spoke of golf, or agreed on points of dogma. During the Vatican Council debates, he had begun to teeter in his contentment. But those stirrings had been just that: circular, without any real momentum; the cleaving to the Latin, for example, rang of disdain for the congregants. Margaret was now giving shape to his misgivings, lending them a vector which they hadn't previously possessed.

He wondered at what she might look like, in a set of vestments, blessing babies. She would be radiant, he knew. He pictured her in the collar, her hair grey but still long and fastened high on her head, wisps coming loose, pearls in her ears. He pictured her dancing at some parish party, wearing slim black trousers and pointed heeled shoes. She would be so very good at that.

Her clavicles lay at gentle angles from her neck.

Where would it all end? he thought.

Really, he already knew.

Mrs Cooper scrubbed the stain. She had been the housekeeper here for thirty years, and she had seen many priests come and go.

22

1964

Now she called him by his first name. Her eyes glinted with the disregard of it. She tacked it on at the end of a sentence: comma, David. He hadn't heard that name spoken by someone outside of his family in quite some time by then. It startled him, made him feel somehow exposed. A challenge he was not expecting. But he liked, ultimately, the way she held it in her mouth.

One evening, she offended him badly.

– Isn't the priesthood an open invitation to the psychologically disturbed, who might be drawn by the prospect of wielding a power and influence beyond challenge, which they feel they are inadequate to win for themselves elsewhere in society? she said, and again he was stunned by her ready-made eloquence. – It leaves the door wide open for the emotionally arrested and provides the perfect bolthole. Unhappily, many cases go undetected until some years after ordination. The most fortunate end up being sorted out in the psychiatrist consulting room, she was saying. – The Church blindly encourages men to adopt a course involving lifelong celibacy. The Church herself lacks the technique of adequately enabling or helping men to achieve this, nor does she help them properly when they fail! She spoke then of a priest she had heard of, it was a story like countless others he'd heard before. The priest had been caught siphoning off the communion wine, too much, as it happened, and had to be admitted to hospital. But his bishop stressed that he be admitted incognito, that if it became known he was a priest, it would discredit them all. There were so many stories like this, David thought ruefully, that the point was moot, but no matter.

– If they put a foot wrong, she was saying, and there are so many ways they can put a foot wrong, they are sent to rot in some backwater of the diocese.

– Is that what you think of me? he said quietly.

She seemed to slow. – No, she said pensively. But I do wonder. What made you choose this?

They said other things to one another, in his house at night, the window giving its ember square to the dark; things which would fall out of her body years later, as she took her slow leave of life.

23

– It's my birthday next week.

He was turning forty.

He lit a cigarette.

They were in his kitchen, had just eaten pork chops with fennel. He stood with his back to the sink.

– What would you like to do?

She asked it as if she was asking the most habitual question in the world, as if they were in a marriage entering its second decade and had hit their stride within it.

– I want to go to the beach. With you.

The words had slipped from the gap between the unsaid and the said. But she was nonplussed.

– Where can we go to the beach from here? she asked.

He visualized the A–Z of Great Britain lying in the boot of his car.

– I don't know. We could take the train. Make a day of it.

– All right.

He experienced her agreement as an escalation; it made him suddenly nervous. Of course he couldn't blame her for calling his bluff. Which hadn't been a bluff. This was something he liked very much in her. She was straight-talking, where he had never known anyone else to be. The unpredictability of this quality was exciting to him. He tried to accord this adjective a sexual neutrality it did not, in this context, possess. He occupied himself with small things in his field of vision. A crack in the paint. The face of the clock. The hangnail hinging from his thumb.

The small train chugged towards the sea. They alighted to the smell of it, a languid stench which David responded to by untensing his whole body, from the knotted muscles of his neck to the arches of his feet. He remembered long days with his family on holiday in Pembrokeshire or Cornwall, playing cricket (wet sand was best, for the bounce), days of running, being cold and wet, then suddenly the supreme pleasure of being warm and dry, his mother wrapping him in a scratchy blanket and rubbing his upper arms until his skin hummed, warm tea from a flask, scones with great peaks of clotted cream. No other web of pleasures could have been clearer to him. He had been innocent then and he felt innocent now, he was sure of it. There was a flicker inside him but he couldn't see the shape of it, or refused. He had in fact packed swimming trunks, but they were stuffed, as if carelessly, down in the bottom of a side pocket.

They agreed to begin with lunch in a pub. They found one tucked down an alley, sufficiently picturesque, with an outdoor area in a brick-walled garden dotted with the vestiges of an orchard: ancient apple trees which drooped in the hot haze of the day. They ate, of course, fish and chips. They agreed, laughing, how much this dish had been missed in Rome, the beer in the batter not so much tasted as smelled, the struggle to describe the appeal of mushy peas to an Italian. They reminisced about the food in Rome. Gelato flavours they had tasted, Margaret asking earnestly if he had been allowed to eat it in the street (the answer was 'Only if I had it in a cup, with a spoon'), beautiful cuts of veal and cured meats, cheese! Olives. Their awe and glee when they learnt that each evening drink came with snacks in tiny steel bowls (she on a rooftop terrace near the Spanish Steps when she had just arrived, racily alone, with a book; him having been taken to some basement place by an older seminarian). They marvelled again at how they'd been to some of the same places at years' remove from one another. Attendant thoughts hovered over them.

After lunch, they caught a bus to the beach, sitting on the top deck, confronted with the oddity of sitting side by side. They'd been opposite one another always, even on the train; now here they were, thighs scrupulously not touching. At times they spoke to one another animatedly, smiling and nodding; at others they caught the shiver of what they were doing and looked forward, or out of the window. The land was fraying from fields into pale sand. Then it was their stop and they were absorbed with making it look like they weren't running the final stretch through the dunes.

The great tent of the afternoon was upon them and they were within it, reading in rented deckchairs.

Next to her in his deckchair striped in mustard and red, David reclined with John Steinbeck. The beach rolled out on either side of them, a generous cream expanse, and out of it, here and there, rose tufts of long dune grass, emerald green. David's hair was windswept, blown into a shape like a cresting wave, honey-coloured. Thinning at his temples and grey beginning to show. The weather of the day moved over the discus of his jaw.

Her own book lay abandoned across her knees, an orange copy of *The Grapes of Wrath*. She wore a spotted sundress, with cap sleeves and narrow lapels. She moved her self-awareness over her body, on what she must look like. Her sandals were red, with crossover straps.

Her hair was up in a French twist, and it wasn't until she thought of it with satisfaction (it had taken her the longest time to master it) that she realized her scalp was aching with the pull of it. Not thinking too hard, she reached up and pulled out her hairslide (a sturdy oval of imitation tortoiseshell). Immediately her hair unspooled on the easterly breeze, great hammered brass wisps of it suddenly dancing at an angle from her head, and to a sudden flash of too-late alarm, onto the side of David's face. Her hair was certainly long, but it emphasized (another flash of something, not quite shock, but being caught at something) how close they had been sitting (who had moved their chair closer in the sand, making it look like an accident, an adjustment?). Her hair moved across him from cheek to temple and back, whipping between his glasses and his eye. It took all of a second. She turned to him in sudden panic, trying to paw back the overspilling strands. He turned to look at her (was that the beginning of a smile?), trapping her hair in the left hinge of his glasses as he did so, and raised a hand to brush it away. She yelped with the pain of the pull in his turning and simultaneously flushed with the sight of his fingers, momentarily, in her hair. She felt the shift in tension, and it ran into her scalp with a fizz. Then it was over, they were tangled, they jumped to their feet, books falling into the sand, and he took his glasses off and stood very close to her, trying to untangle them. In the end she took the glasses from him and pulled the hair loose. The golden threads, broke, frizzed unpleasantly at their broken ends.

– Would you like to go for a swim? He had worked his way up to this question.

There was nothing to fear. Swimming was one of life's great pleasures. Besides, everyone was made gawky by the water. But the last word half-died in his throat, betraying an intention unvoiced.

– Can't, I'm afraid. Margaret smiled at him. – Scarlet fever when I was twelve. Can't get my ears wet. But I can join you for a paddle.

Suddenly shy. Swimming only worked if it was an activity of reciprocal exposure. To his distress he felt a blush rushing up his face. His ears boomed with it. He looked around for a changing hut like the ones which used to pepper the beaches of his youth and saw to his horror that there were none. It was too early in the season. What to do? Every other place he'd ever been he hadn't had to think about it. But those had been clean white rooms of tile and steam full of boys or men, and Margaret was a woman. He couldn't think what women did. He refused to believe their rituals were the same as his, wandering as one among many blunt statements of bodies, their towels coming away without a thought. At the English College they'd all changed in their rooms before wandering the halls half-naked to get to the pool; it had been the same at the Palazzola.

His thinking flicked with panic from the prospect of changing in front of Margaret under a towel (he wasn't sure how that would work) to running back into town and asking to use the bathroom in the pub where they'd been earlier. But that involved a bus ride and the mercy of its timetable. He must have looked suddenly alarmed, because Margaret suggested he go find a 'secluded dune'. She was already unbuckling her shoes. Her toenails, painted red, were neat and fine. He thought for a moment what it would be like to run his thumb over them. He took off his glasses and went.

When he returned she had made a small pile of their possessions and was waiting for him, her skirts already gathered up in her hands. She was smiling at him and this knocked at him a moment, but he made a show of running towards her. His shorts were cobalt blue.

From behind the shelter of her sunglasses, she looked him up and down, quickly so she could convince herself she hadn't done it. There was a sharp line of tan at his neck and the rest of him was pale as limestone. He had a visible notch in one of his collarbones from it having been broken; she presumed this was a rugby injury, so common in boys of his background (the scrum, the blood-thickened snap of it like a twig). He had a thin fan of hair, spread pleasingly even over a tight chest (his nipples flat and unassuming). His stomach held a central column of muscle which travelled down to a tidy, tight lower lip on the navel (a comet-thought streaked: which party would it please more if it were to be licked), gathered round with pale, glinting down. He had gorgeous legs.

Years later she would find the dress she wore that day. The pockets when she put her hands into them were still gritted with sand.

He ran straight into the froth of it, while she picked her way slowly, like some long-legged bird, and bunched her skirts up higher and higher. Soon they were up past her knees and she was shrieking in delight. He turned to grin at her. He choked on his laugh and then on the surf, he slipped, fell over, went under, filled his nose with salt. He came up and she was over him, reaching her hand and wrist with the delicate black-strapped watch down to his shoulder, asking him laughingly if he was all right. The crow's feet of her eyes alight with mirth and concern. He saw, not for the first time, the smattering of freckles across her nose.

They were quiet on the train home. As they slowed to pull into the station he got up and walked the length of several carriages, descending onto the platform at a distance to her. They walked on opposite sides of the street until their paths diverged, him to the presbytery, her to the college. She angled herself quickly to smile at him, and turned up the garden path. Her hair caught the early spring's descending sunlight as if it were wild honey held in a jar. He was reminded, briefly, of that line in *A Farewell to Arms*, when Catherine undoes the pins of her hair and it falls around them both, *like a curtain*. He wondered at that cloistered intimacy; to have a woman's arms around you, and her legs around you, and her hair all around like a thing to keep you safe and unseen.

He swept the thought aside.

24

SHE LENT HIM her copy of *Silent Spring*. He read it quickly, knowing that at the end she would be waiting, wanting to talk to him about it. He anticipated her face readying itself, her hands and their repertoire of gestures.

They were in his sitting room at night. All the trees blading in their new leaf. A stack of graded papers, clipped, on the coffee table between them. He turned his pen in his hands. She lamented the lack of a more prominent Christian environmentalist movement.

– Yes, he said. It seems there is an excellent opportunity for us to lead in this area.

– Look upon the earth and let it cherished be.

– Exactly.

– God's house is the world before it is the church.

– I think part of the problem is the persistence of eschatology.

Sometimes she did this. Turned out perfect sentences that belonged in a book, not mouthed in a conversation taking place in a kitchen, late at night, on an unassuming Tuesday in May. Which startled him. She wore her thoughts on her face, and never sought to hide or alloy them. They had known each other a year now. He asked her what she meant.

– If we think there is another life, she said, what is the point of this one, other than to try and earn our place in the next? And conversely (*Conversely*, he thought. Who else had she spoken to like this?), if Judgement Day is a finite event, then there is no need to try and stave off this gradual poisoning of the earth, the decimation of all that creep and crawl upon it. She spoke like scripture, he realized, though it was obvious, with a referential pleasure. All those notes she told him of, in her days at Regina Mundi. The Gospel of Luke, the shewings of Julian. – We must denounce them, she was saying now, our out-of-date ideas about the end of the world. It won't end. It will winnow down. The earth will be left a pallid, scorched, impoverished thing.

He tried to say something about the nuclear threat, but he could tell that she wasn't interested in this, she was already pivoting back. – What if, instead, we treated this life as heaven? *Heaven is at hand*? That we have to find it, make it for ourselves. Work as if we were already living in the early days of a better world.

He had the sense, once more, of her straying into territory he had never known anyone to walk before. Of course, he knew that there were currents, here and abroad, of exactly this kind of thinking, but he had never found it so embodied. And now here was this woman, sitting with her legs crossed on his sofa, beckoning him into foreign fields. He topped up her glass of sherry. There was a small ladder in her left stocking.

– Do you not find, she said, that Catholic relic worship is

quite out of step with many of the other Abrahamic faiths' attitudes to mortal remains?

– Go on.

– Well, chopping people into bits and putting them on display.

They reminisced for a moment about the most lurid relics they could think of. The section of John the Baptist's head looking like a swimming cap, or a rugby ball. Thomas's probing finger.

– But reliquaries are interesting.

– Oh?

– Some of them have an irony.

She evoked the ones she spoke of as a Northern European phenomenon, mostly: Limoges, Cologne, Bruges. – They are shaped like buildings. Church naves in miniature. Maquettes, she said. Which begs the question: if the reliquaries and churches mirror each other, the reliquary housing the relics and the churches housing us, then are we also holy proof of a kind? Are our bodies not the matter of miracles? What is it that is being enshrined?

25

He introduced her to Ralph.

They were in the pub. Ralph was there with a friend, who gave her a cursory look and then launched into telling them about how a man in the village – a carpenter and a regular at this very pub, in fact – had broken off his engagement in order to live with another man in a cottage on the outskirts. David listened, tense, and watched Margaret flex her wrists over the table. He didn't know what she would say, but he knew it would be devastatingly concise, and would rearrange the frames of his thinking once more.

Ralph had drained his pint, and David could see he wanted another. The friend's disgust was reaching its crescendo now. – I just dread to think what they do in bed, he said, shuddering. He took a long sip of beer with his eyes shut.

– Then don't. Margaret's voice was cool. – Just as I don't want to imagine what you do in bed, or you me.

Ralph put his pint down abruptly. He shot David a hard look. The friend sucked his stout and coughed.

– Besides, many couples use anal sex as a way of avoiding pregnancy.

Ralph turned to David wide-eyed. David offered what he knew was a conciliatory grin. The friend who, it was now obvious, was bluntly drunk, merely got up and walked away, patting his pockets in some pretence of having forgotten something. Ralph called after him half-heartedly, but then pivoted back on his barstool and looked Margaret up and down. – Where on earth did you come from? He laughed.

David and Margaret walked home together in the dark. David began to talk, and Margaret sensed the smoothing out of some great intimacy, which only being side by side would permit.

– When we were at school, he began. Inside her shoes, her feet shifted and clenched. Her arms were resolutely crossed.

– There were two boys. And older and a younger. They were caught. Doing things.

Here he paused to check Margaret's understanding. In her peripheral vision she saw him turn and search her profile.

– Go on.

– They called a whole school assembly. I was in a middle year. Ralph was in the last year of the junior school.

– They called the older one up on stage.

Row upon row of boys in blazers of baby blue, breathing together.

– Father Porter stood at the lectern and told us all what they'd done. Or he told us without telling us.

Porter had used all the predictable words, spitting them out as if he were skimming stones. He rocked on his heels. He gripped the lectern. The boy stood there, fixing his gaze upon a vague point at the far end of the hall. Ralph was in the same year as the younger boy they'd caught. Simmonds was his name. Father Porter wasn't naming him now, but the boys knew; they'd found Simmonds and asked him about it, and he'd told them readily and in detail. The boys had crowded round his bed, going steadily slack-jawed with horror. Simmonds was odd, and guileless, and his descriptions were delivered very matter-of-factly. Simmonds wasn't here now. His parents had come to collect him, his father looking like a cliff face and his mother looking anxious. They'd driven him away and none had gathered to watch him go. Later he would be killed at El Alamein.

In the hall, the older boy wriggled under the hot inquisitive gaze of his peers. David thought he seemed quite pitiable, no chair to sit on (the masters, as usual, sat in a loose semicircle towards the back of the stage), no lectern to grip or to lean on. He had tried to put his hands into his blazer pockets, but Father Porter broke off his tirade (he had moved on to telling the room that this would be the downfall of the country, *this* was the reason they were losing India, *this* was the worm in the rose, the rot which needed, urgently, to be rooted out). He screamed at the boy, the tendons of his neck jumping against the starch of his collar: Keep those filthy hands where we can see them, boy!

David saw that there was movement elsewhere on the stage. One of the masters had appeared from behind the screen. He was holding something, a long thin object. It was resting across his two hands, which were palm-up, at right angles to his body.

Margaret said, under her breath, Oh no.

David had stopped now, in the parasol of jaundiced light under a lamppost, and was staring stiffly at the ground.

– They made him turn around. The boy. And they told him

to undo his belt, and drop his trousers and his undergarments round his ankles.

Margaret felt the walls of her throat coming together. The queasy primness of *undergarments* made some rush of instinct come up inside her, some desire to soothe him. They had stopped walking. She was standing apart from him, in the shadows, and she had the sense of herself hovering ineffectually, like a lint-winged moth.

David still remembered the wiry gold hair on the boy's buttocks. The master had flicked the whip on each of the boy's thighs to make him part his legs, then handed it to Father Porter. The boy was made to lean forward on a chair which had now been placed in front of him. The lilac of his scrotum came into view. Years later, when he closed his eyes, David would remember how it shook in the minutes which followed. Like petals, pelted by rain.

– They made us count, David said. He took off his glasses and polished them badly on his jumper. Something to give his fingers to do. – All of us. They made us count aloud, louder and louder, all the way to thirty.

At first the boys were reticent, begrudging in their volume, but then the boy began to scream in pain, and so they began trying to outdo themselves, to hide his voice with theirs. By the end of it, they were all hoarse. Silence fell in the hall. Father Porter was breathing heavily.

– Oh no, Margaret said again. She wanted to reach out to him, to touch him in some small way, some gesture towards the feminized comfort she knew women were supposed to provide, but to do so felt too deliberate. That day at the beach, when she had plunged her hand in to pull him up, had had its proper pretext. This, somehow, did not. And it was too late now, he was shrugging, repositioning his glasses on his nose, moving on under the fulsome summer leaves and past the slick black fences where foxes wove with their trickster snouts. *Warped* was the word which throbbed warmly in her mind, as the tempo of her shoes picked up and she followed him. There was something closed now about him, visible in his shoulders. They walked side by side and said nothing.

Not long afterwards, Ralph asked both of them over for Sunday lunch. His wife Anna was postponing usual lunchtime hours for their benefit. Margaret had gone to David's Mass so that they could drive over together afterwards. She sat in a row near the front and when he'd seen the last of the regulars out of the door, he motioned with his chin to the vestry. She followed him in, and found there was nowhere to sit down. She leant against a window frame and tried not to watch him remove his vestments. There was the cassock underneath, smooth over his chest but hiding the shapes of his legs. He asked for her opinion on his homily and she gave it, frankly. He smiled at her in the mirror over the washbasin while he soaped his hands. She was wearing a green dress with a wide clean neckline that skimmed her collarbones, long sleeves with covered buttons at the cuffs, and a thin matching belt. It was a good dress for church, and a good dress for meeting Anna in, he thought. Anna would like it, and he wanted Anna to like her, although, if asked, he would not really have been able to say why. – You look eminently presentable, he said, and she smiled.

When they pulled up outside the house, one of the younger sons, Jonah, was playing in the front garden – some game involving ants and bits of broken twig. He turned when he heard the car approaching and began to jump up and down. When Margaret got out of the car, moving her handbag to the crook of her arm, he said:

– Hello. Who are you?

Margaret folded into a squat so she could be level with him, and replied, – My name is Margaret. What's yours? She ungloved her hand and held it out to him. His chin was tucked in emphatically, but he took the five tips of her fingers in his little hand and moved them up and down.

– I am Jonah.

– It's very nice to meet you, Jonah.

– Why are you here?

– I am friends with your uncle. I'm here to have lunch with all of you. What are you doing?

– The ants need help. With their motorway.

– Oh yes? And how are you helping them?

David watched as Jonah took Margaret's hand again, and led her over to the lavender border. She leant over and exclaimed over Jonah's efforts. She asked him questions. They looked at the ants together. Jonah pointed and Margaret nodded. Then Ralph opened the door and moved out onto the doorstep and clapped his hands in emphatic welcome. Anna was just making the Yorkshire puddings. Margaret walked through the house to where the sounds and smells of cooking were.

– Hello.

Anna turned, a bowl held against her lower middle, moving a spoon through it.

– Hello!

The two women looked at each other. There was a small child sucking its thumb and holding a fistful of Anna's dress.

Margaret stood in the doorway. Anna's eyes were warm, and the flushed skin of her cheeks was pushed up onto high proud bones. Margaret saw a happy woman she hoped would be her friend. Her eyes moved to where the additional aprons hung, and she went to tie one round herself.

In the front room, the men drank gin and French.

The summer came and went. Margaret stayed with Giovanni in Tuscany for the duration: long days of reading and sleep. David took his two weeks in July, and went cycling in Normandy with Mack. They did not speak of her.

Margaret and David exchanged letters at studiously appropriate intervals, filled with questions about the next term's teaching, what they were reading. Nothing more.

26

THE AUTUMN LEAVES had already bedded well into their own rotting when Margaret came up against a new obstacle in her teaching.

She'd been looking at the Annunciation with her students, as it is described, most famously, in Luke: *How can this be, since I know not a man?*

– Ladies, said Margaret, making a gathering gesture of her arms, there are two words in this passage I would like us to consider. Firstly, this *know*. What can we assume Mary knows of carnal knowledge? Does she mean she has never been left alone with a man? Does she know how babies are made? Secondly, this *overshadow. And the angel answering, said to her: The Holy Ghost shall come upon thee, and the power of the most High shall overshadow thee.* From the Greek, to shade; meaning also to envelop in a haze. It sounds menacing, like *overpower*. With the latter it sounds much like the ether of our obstetric methods today. Is it possible that Luke is making deliberate reference to the conception of Perseus by Danae in Greek myth, who was impregnated by Zeus taking the form of a highly localized shower of golden rain?

(She chuckled to herself.) This is ejaculate as narcotic, as crop spray.

Row upon row of young women turned their coin-bright faces to her.

– Miss? What is that?

Margaret's hands had been moving off again into a grander gesture as she gained momentum. Now they fell back to the desk, where she leant forward.

– Ejaculate?

The student, whose name was Amelia, nodded. Margaret scanned the other faces of the room. They looked back blankly.

Margaret looked down at her hands. A choice now presented itself: give them the discreet, disjointed information, as she had been given; or right the wrongs of their ignorance, of her own as it had been handed to her, and tell them everything. She looked up again. Her students were twenty years old or thereabouts. They had come out of the convent schools of their towns, in so many cases the best schools in their areas. Some of them born-and-bred Catholics; others like her: bright, and taken in by it all. If she told them, she knew, the hammer would fall hard upon her. Best to tell them, then, what no other would.

– You have probably heard of seed? A man's seed?

Some nodded slowly. Others shook their heads.

So she spent the rest of the lesson telling them about their bodies. She drew different contraceptive methods on the blackboard. She told them about abortion and the state of a foetus at different stages. She told them about pleasure and spoke of its importance.

– I am telling you this because I think no one else has told you these things before. Please make of this information what you will. But you are soon to move out into your lives and some of you will meet and marry quickly, and then you will want control over when – and if – the babies come.

She told David that same evening. He looked aghast.
 – This will come back to bite you.
 – So be it.
 – You are endangering your prospects.
 – I have other prospects.
There was a silence. Opera had been playing, *Carmen*, but now the needle bobbed on the record. David sat up straight and sighed. Margaret was all chin and challenge, resting her fingers on her knees.
 – Doesn't it make you tired, David?
He let fly his question with a look.
 – All of this cover-up? This effort to keep people in such ignorance of their own plumbing?
Plumbing. He liked that. Why was she so good at that?
 – It's starting to wear on me, you know. It feels like so much . . . bad translation.
He had said nothing for a time. She began to talk, not looking at him.
 – When I was a girl I was given no information about my body. My own self. It was only when I got to university and I met someone. She was rubbing her hand on the space beneath her collarbones, as if to calm a cantering heart. – An older man, ex-Navy, and he explained it to me. You have to remember I was an only child, I had never seen a naked man, or boy, before. Of course there were paintings, but really nothing prepares you for the first time you see an erection.

David, unprepared, started visibly at this. Somewhere in the bowl of his pelvis, a knot pulled itself to.

– And then the pleasure. The pleasure of it felt so esoteric, arcane. Or else some fluke I'd fallen upon. The first time I had an orgasm I thought there was a bleed on my brain, I thought I was dying. Which explains the joke, as I later learnt.

There was nothing he could say. He thought dimly of Marie, on the narrow back bench of her car, in falling snow.

– My parents were so . . . prim about these things. I think if I'd been a boy, my father the engineer would have taken a much more structural, pragmatic approach. He would have used (she laughed ruefully) a hydraulic analogy. She paused and picked a piece of lint from her leg. – But the pleasure felt like a cover-up, and then seeking it out became its own insurrection.

David could picture it all too well: Margaret aged nineteen, setting her sights on someone at a party. Looking back at a man with those eyes, their many colours of maritime storms. Margaret smoothing the pale straps of her slip from her bare (freckled?) shoulders. Margaret flexing her wrists as she woke in someone else's bed. He shook his head gently.

– I am afraid. For you.

– Don't be. I'm a member of the union.

By noon the next day all the nuns knew. There was no point asking herself how.

As they took their places in the refectory for lunch, Margaret saw the wimples waving out of the corners of her eyes. She clasped her hands and inclined her head, waiting for the grace. She wished David were here to sit across from. She tried to meet the eyes of some of the novices and supplicants. They shot short shy smiles at her, even as their worried eyes moved towards high table and the more senior sisters. Some of her students nodded solemnly, appreciatively, she hoped. Sister Augusta came in late, located Margaret, and walked to where she stood.

– Come with me, Miss Bendelow. I would speak with you.
– Now?
– Yes. Now.

The shifting creak of a floorboard in the hall. Margaret nodded in acquiescence and followed Sister Augusta out of the room.

In her office, Sister Augusta spread her hands over the desk.

– Close the door.

Then:

– Can you explain yourself?

Margaret gathered her reserve. – I should say, Sister Augusta, that I believe very strongly in what we are all doing here.

– Do you now?
– Yes. I so enjoy being a part of your community.

Sister Augusta cocked an eyebrow.

– Is that so?
– Yes.
– Then why, Miss Bendelow? Why on earth—
– We have an opportunity, I think, to be at the cutting edge of Catholic education here and I wish we would seize it, said Margaret. For all our sakes.
– Explain.
– I believe, Sister, that if Catholicism is to be a vivifying

force in our society, in the future, then what we need is for its women to have a high degree of self-knowledge. Family and marriage not as the drudgery of the factory floor, of production, but of vocation in the truest sense. With its proper ecstasies.

Sister Augusta cocked an incredulous eyebrow.

– What you *believe* is not the question. Her look like thunder. – The question is, how *dare* you do this to us?

– To you?

– You, Miss Bendelow, are a snake. I have spoken to Archbishop Dwyer about this, and, let me tell you, he is *incensed*. He will speak with you himself.

– Why not Father Fletcher?

– What about him?

– Isn't he my most immediate superior? Shouldn't he be having a word with me?

– He declined to meet with you on this matter. I would not presume to speculate as to his reasoning.

– What do you mean?

– You are within my jurisdiction. He is not.

– Why not? If our roles were reversed, and he had told them what I told them yesterday, would you be punishing him?

– Miss Bendelow, do not play the fool with me. It doesn't suit you. He would never.

– I want you to say it, though. Say it. Say that he is a man and I'm a woman, and that's why you are punishing me.

– Miss Bendelow! He is not a *man*. He is a priest. Now get out.

27

– Your employment, Miss Bendelow, was an experiment. It would be a pity were it to fail so soon.

She had been driven to Dwyer's office by Sister Michael, whom she knew was sitting outside listening.

– Are you suggesting that it was always destined to fail, my being here? It has just been a matter of when?

He opens his hands in a resigned gesture.

– When Professor Jones wrote to refer you to us, he sang your praises.

Jones had been a lecturer at Regina Mundi. A craggy man of many tangents.

Dwyer continued.

– I consulted with Sister Augusta and we agreed that it was worth giving you a go. If only to see for ourselves what all the fuss was about with the women's theology college. We knew that a parish over in Coventry had taken on one of your predecessors, class of fifty-six, and were delighted with her. But Sister Augusta and I agreed that we'd give you a year. And it seems we must leave it at two. Your contract will be terminated at the end of the academic year in order to minimize disruption for the students. You will be paid through the summer, which I think is generous, under the circumstances. I must say, though, that I did not expect this. And with Father Fletcher too, who is one of my best. You are a thief in the orchard, Miss Bendelow, and I will not let you take him from us.

Here Margaret's mind snagged.

– I'm afraid I don't follow. What has he got to do with this? I taught this lesson without him. He was not present. He didn't know I was going to do it.

– You and I both know, Miss Bendelow, that your relationship with Father Fletcher is somewhat less than professional. Dwyer had inclined his chin slightly.

– What are you implying? Margaret pulled her posture to.

– You know very well, my child.

Thus it came to be that David was told he was being transferred to another parish. It was to be his punishment: she had the protection of employment law, he did not.

He was summoned to the episcopal offices on a Wednesday. A red-carpeted room. An enormous dark desk carved with mullioned arches, inlaid with crimson leather. Dwyer stood at it, with his hands spread. Before David could open his mouth it had begun.

– Word has reached my ears, Fletcher. His stance at the desk like a schoolmaster's. The sisters are concerned. I am told you have been spending much more time *conspiring* with this Miss Bendelow. A disgusted waving of the hand. An enormous amethyst shone on his finger.

– She and I work together.

– In your house? At night?

– We are marking.

– Well, you mark me, Fletcher, no good will come of this.

There was a long pause. Things roiled in it. The tide of David's blood rushed, then dimmed in his ears.

– You are being transferred. I am sending you to another parish.

– Which one?

– Burslem. St Joseph's. You are to have no more contact with Miss Bendelow.

– When?

– Immediately.

– Why?

– The current priest has been taken ill quite suddenly. Needs to spend some time in one of our treatment centres.

– Is there no one else?

– Enough, Fletcher. You know how it is. Where the need is greatest.

David went home and lay on his back on his bed trying to breathe. Margaret would come later that evening, presuming the usual. When she rang the bell, he would walk the length of his hallway in the dark, clutching at things to say and ways to say them. She would be a shape on the other side of the glass, and then a real woman, moving past him into the space, bringing with her smells of the quotidian outdoors, of rain and fresh earth and damp clothes and leather and waterproofing wax. She would remove her outermost layers and hang them on a long line of hooks made for such a purpose. There would be a silk scarf knotted under her chin to protect her hair, and as she would untie it he would catch the finest whisper of her perfume.

She will go to his drinks cabinet and mix herself a drink and sip it and sigh and sit on his sofa. She will look at him expectantly, exultantly. She will ask him how his day went, a rote intimacy which he will now be barred from.

And he will tell her. He will assume the pose he has been trained to adopt when delivering difficult news: seated opposite, knees slightly apart (gently expansive, assertive), hands moving from clasped to steepled, gesturing open and then coming together again, head inclined at a gentle downward left. It is a pose which is both solicitous and withholding. It offers tempered comfort and authority.

While he tells her she will sit very still. For a few moments something will fall away from her face, but then she will put her drink down very softly, on its coaster, and will nod once, with an emphasis he knows she hopes will be foreclosing. She will rise without saying anything and move back into the hall. He will hear her putting her arms back into the sleeves of her coat and the metallic sounds of her closing herself back into it. He will rouse himself to get up, lean in the doorway (his hands, shaking, in his pockets), looking at the pinned twist of her hair. The sound of the lock in the latch will be sad.

Margaret walked back up the hill in the dark. The sky, seen through the cedar branches, was speckled as the shell of an egg with stars.

She had felt in his house that there was a choice to be made between dignity and truth, and she had chosen dignity. When he explained it to her, the ripostes rose in her wildly, but she saw also that they would be no use. She was a force, but she was not, after all, unstoppable, and she had met her object and flung herself against it, and no one would even remember she had done so. She must not delude herself: she was a martyr to no cause. He was their creature, a creature of authority and hierarchy, and she was just a woman. She was thirty-seven, and inside her there was a space the size of a clenched fist which she had neither filled nor forsworn. She wished now that she could have chosen an announced purpose for it, and stuck to it. She hated his training and his contrived performance of wisdom (the hands moving under his words). She hated these higher-up men calcified by lack of life and absence of soul. She hated that these were their intentions for his soul; his soul which was so interesting to her.

She stopped at the benches where they had first met. She bit a callous on her thumb.

She reminded herself that she had been anticipating one such man, a man of cramped and curtailed soul, when she'd met him. Instead he had come striding towards her shining with his vocation. It was visible in every muscle of his face. She'd never seen another like him, so lit with his life. Well, maybe Tristan, she conceded to herself. Tristan had had a light too, and she had loved it in him, a love that made her lie down on a dust sheet on a bare concrete floor once a week.

Had that been dignity?

The buildings of the college leaked their institutional lighting into the darkness of the garden.

Margaret felt the truth come on.

His soul was interesting to her.

It was precious and it was being wasted.

It was a waste not because he was a beautiful man living alone in a house with too many coat hooks.

It was a waste because of what they woke in one another.

She had been searching all her life for this, in every space. To be so besouled of another.

She wanted to live under the arc of his laugh for ever.

28

2019

THERE WERE THINGS which she never told anyone, which she kept locked in the reliquary of herself, which were now being shaken loose, like pearls. They were thrown from her like lint, nutshells; garden waste. Adrian caught what he could.

She remembered finding sand in the pockets of a dress years after she had last worn it. The sand spilling from another coast onto the floor of a new life.

She remembered a stonemason, who had been, perhaps, was he, her husband?

She found, to her discomfort, that her body remembered him. Her bowel and her solar plexus and her throat. She remembered the ease with which his hands moved through the shadows of their making. He had had a young wife who had not been her, and she lived in warm butter colours, a tastefully lit life of sconces and lamps. Whereas she, Margaret, had gone down in the shadows, the granular shadows of granite or limestone; the plum-coloured strata of slate. Their sex had been so immediately easy and good. Knowledge of this had hung over them like an omen in flames.

The last time she saw him he had unzipped her dress and smoothed it away over her back.

No. Think not of that.

Now and again, descendants and carers floated in and out of her field of vision, like hands.

She remembered a wedding and afterwards. His gentleness. His timidity. How she'd tried, once, to go on top but face away, and then she'd felt self-conscious, had made a noise of uncertainty, and he had said come back, had brought her in close, kissed her, said no, that wasn't very nice, come back, stay close, I want to see your face, I love your face.

She had loved his face too. Its startlingly typical beauty. His gorgeous laconic grin.

There is bread yet to be broken and love yet to be made.

Quoting Martin Luther was a cliché, but she had done it once.

Another had said to her: you're the first woman I've met to have a mind of her own.

It was the truth and she tried not to make excuses for it.

She'd had one child. Or was it three?

The hospital in Tripoli was run by nuns. Italians. Some imperial hangover, their presence.

The local boys hunted gazelles for sport. When they could, the nuns found them and rescued them, kept them in the walled garden, fed them dates and hard grasses. They grew fat, flicking their tails over their creamy hinds, lowering their lashes languidly.

When her husband had his first heart attack, he'd fallen out of bed and she'd been woken. In the night. The floor was boards, and her first thought was that he would be cold. She could not let this happen. She had made vows to that effect, in some neat room, in a cold city she'd never much cared for. She dragged him onto the carpet and covered him with the blanket from the bed. She called the ambulance from the kitchen telephone and lay down next to him, to wait until it arrived.

In hospital recovering he'd become hooked on *The Archers*.

The second heart attack had been when they were in another place. Was it this place, where she sat now? Perhaps. It had been before dawn, in the summer. Their daughter was home from boarding school. She found him, and he had sent her to get the priest. He came, wearing jeans and a faded Provençal shirt. On his feet he had espadrilles. Margaret knew that her husband had told him the whole story, and it was the first time he had spoken it to anyone. What passed between the two men, he would never tell her, but afterwards he started going to Mass again. She would not come with him.

– Will you love me for ever?
– I shall do my best.

Her hands are stilled now to think of it. His face then had been one of a child's. She had wanted to hold it, and had; had wanted then to hold him in the cup of herself for ever.

And could she say she had done her best, each and every day of their life? His life?

She thought of the thousand ways they had shown their love to one another, and been unnoticed, or else misapprehended. Cups of tea in their multitudes. Crooked inventions of his to ease her in her pastimes. The plank full of nails bent at an angle, for her spools of thread. The bookshelves, made from salvaged floorboards. The gardens, where each year, across new houses in often harsh climates, he coaxed from the earth roses and jasmine, herbs and flame-flowered pomegranate trees. Thick cool shade for her to read in. Sunday roasts. Drinks mixed and brought to her desk. Records played, and dancing. So much dancing. Long drives, late at night, to fetch one another from this or that place. Jumpers knitted. Quilts stitched, spread over both of their knees on winter evenings. Reading to one another. Paintings they had stood before, side by side, and agreed that they were mawkish, or gory, or transcendentally affecting. All that love, all that labour, made and unmade. Her love had gone under the high green oak. Somewhere it all played on, riffing on itself, creating endless variations.

She no longer thought that people could be saved by others. She had wanted to save him. Or else, he had believed she could, and his belief weighed too heavily on her. The task had been too much. He had asked too much of her. He had wanted her to be too many things. Or else she had not, in the end, been up to it.

She had lived in his love. Had known its sureness. She had sworn all the living minutes of her life to him, had given them gladly, and then he had died and left her alone in this twilit life for twenty years.

29

1964

BURSLEM WAS A poor inner parish of Stoke-on-Trent. Its parishioners were those who worked in the potteries. The problems they came to him with in confession were ones he felt ill-equipped to deal with: tales of drink and battery, unwanted pregnancy, gambling. They made him nervous.

He felt as if part of his mind was missing.

He longed for the cool precision of her talk and her presence, the lean lines of her draped across his furniture. She was the only person he could really talk to. Only at the English College had he spoken to others like this, without artifice, but not since. She had the habit, he now recognized, of pulling his thoughts into focus, making them known to himself. He conducted conversations with her in his head, writing to her as his hands engaged in other tasks. It was like playing the most expansive game of chess. He put out his thoughts and hoped for her tightening, answering challenge.

These were weeks when rain runnelled over the windows with a cold insistence. The sisters started to bully her. It began small. When they walked past one another, she alone and them always in pairs, their gazes slid over and past her and they did not greet her. Their wimples inclined towards one another in low urgent talk. They no longer spoke to her. But one day she came into her room to find a bloodied sanitary pad under the presser foot of her sewing machine. Her clothes came back from the laundry mysteriously damaged: ripped, stained, buttons gone. At meals she was served conspicuously last, always the scrapings or the last few potatoes in the dish, which had been sitting in now-cold water.

Certain things were set in motion now, and could not be recalled. She knew that to them she was the woman who had wormed her way in and stolen him from his life, from all of them. They watched and waited to make their moves on her, and later she would be sent hence, alone again and with no reference. She called Eileen and asked her what to do.

– Hold your nerve, pet. Do your job. And go out with a bang, I say.

She retreated to her room. The gospels no longer held the hearthlight she had always found in them. Her mind felt dulled, without its dancing partner. Her hands were restless, and she turned with great vehemence to sewing. In defiance, she made herself bright, short things in reds and oranges: a paisley-patterned minidress, scarlet cigarette trousers in which she strode up and down the aisles of her classroom.

Her students sensed a new hardness in her, saw that it was at odds with the hardness of the nuns, and quietly and industriously applied themselves to their work.

At night Margaret lay in her bed and wondered who he had to talk to.

After six weeks, David called Margaret. A high-risk thing to do, but he couldn't chance a letter. Independently of one another, they'd both wondered if Sister Augusta considered herself above intercepting their post. They had separately concluded she was not.

He called the phone in the post room at the college. It was early evening. The porter answered, and grudgingly went off to find Miss Bendelow. David sat at his desk holding his breath. He could hear the returning clip of her shoes.

– Hello? He felt her voice in his feet. It was a small word but a weighty code, he told himself. *Hello* meant I long for you as well, I need you too, this is not for ever, I will sit on your sofa again and be flush with the frustrations of this or that thing. He thought of her, three drinks in, flexing her unshod toes. The careful darning there. He wanted to see how well her heel fit in the palm of his hand.

He told her about his new parishioners, how they scared him: the unwanted children, the bruising marriages, the bottle. – It's awful, he said.

– You only think it's awful because you've never had to acknowledge this kind of problem before.

– But my previous parishioners didn't come to me with things like this.

– That doesn't mean they didn't have the same troubles.

There was a pause. He waited for her to tell him what to do. At her end, she realized that it was their poverty that unsettled him, their desperation and their genuine belief that he could help.

– The woman who didn't want the baby. What did you tell her?

David swallowed. He had a childish sense that whatever he said now would be wrong, and he didn't want it to be. He wanted to dazzle her with his priestly acumen, as he had felt himself to dazzle many others before. He could hear her opening her cigarette case. A series of nonchalant sounds.

– I directed her towards the church's baby bank.

Margaret felt her esteem for him slip. Of course he could have done little else, she told herself. She thought of Rezia. She pictured this other, English, girl, who must have sat, nervous and nauseated, on the other side of the grille, hoping for help. What must she be: six, eight, ten weeks along? Margaret felt herself stretching to parse the gap between them.

– Put her in touch with me.

– Why?

– You don't need to know why.

And that was how it went. Margaret found an abortionist for the woman, whose name was Nora, and accompanied her to the appointment in the offices of a gynaecologist in central Birmingham, who was known to be quick. When it was done, she saw her home to her terraced house and her four children, who were playing in the neighbour's garden. She told them to let their mother rest, she was ill and needed to stay in bed for at least a day; she cooked them a supper of scrambled eggs on toast and did her best to keep them occupied until their father came home from work. Then she got a complicated sequence of trams and buses back to the college.

It was late by the time she arrived, and Sister Augusta curled her lip at her as she passed.

Margaret suggested David start an Alcoholics Anonymous group. He had heard of it, of course, but thought it carried a whiff of American exhibitionism. No, she assured him, it really did work, it was the most effective method yet found to battle alcoholism. She helped him start the group by going to the print shop herself to order and collect the flyers. They went on long walks together, distributing them. She was heading to Birmingham every ten days or so now, and receiving many calls, sometimes late into the evening. She would steal a short distance down the road, where there was a phone box, and then she would stand in its buttery-yellow column of light, her lips moving slowly and illegibly above the receiver. If David called her, she could be seen through the glass of the post-room door, sitting stiffly on the uncomfortable stool, smoothing the hem of her skirt repetitively.

She learnt, through a friend, of a woman who helped battered wives: she ran a network, informally, of mostly widows, who could take in women and their children for a week or two after they left, while they found their feet in new lives. Margaret got this woman's number, and, when David put her in touch with a woman whose husband beat her with belts or wooden spoons or rug beaters, Margaret passed it on. When he expressed wonderment at how rife these issues were in this congregation compared to the first, she corrected him.

– Wife battery is enormous. It's everywhere.
– Then why did I never hear about it in Monks Kirby?
– Money. Money, David.

Before long she was referring women regularly. They didn't

always go, she knew, but she knew also that even a piece of paper with a number scrawled on it was a beam of light breaking into the mineshaft.

One afternoon Margaret herself received a call from the woman who had started this loose constellation of aid. She did not give her name, but she explained, concisely, that someone had done the same for her once, after her husband had attempted to strangle her one Saturday night.

– How did you get this number? Margaret asked cautiously.

– Never mind that. The voice was deep, a smoker's, with a thick Black Country accent. – Who are you?

Margaret did not know how to answer this question. She tucked a stray strand of hair back into her bun.

– I work—it's a bit difficult to explain.
– You know the new priest at St Joseph's, don't you?
– Yes.
– How much does he know about this?
– I try to give him as little information as possible.
– Good.

Margaret could feel the gaze of someone through the glass pane of the door. She turned to look. It was Sister Louisa. Not known for her discretion, nor her accurate understanding of the things she saw.

The voice on the other end of the line said: – Well done, love.

The line clicked cut.

That night Margaret began a new sewing project. It was an item of frivolous glamour: her heart had given a minor lurch at the sight of the fabric, pale green silk, months ago when she was in Stoke on an errand. Without yet knowing what she would make it into, she had bought six yards of it, an extraordinarily extravagant purchase. Now she was making it into a skirt suit. She had dug out the pattern she wanted and had cut out all the requisite pieces.

She pinned the panels of cloth to one another and she thought of her present doings. She felt she had been offered a new place, should she so choose. Here was a life among women which suited her better: not the sequestered sisterhood of the nuns, but in the world, where women toiled and slipped what salvation they could to one another like secret notes. She knew, of course, that there were other orders, elsewhere, in which the nuns moved out into society, having trained as doctors and nurses and midwives, and collaborated with lay professionals, social workers and psychologists, and did thorough, consequential work. But these women were not here, a village in the Birmingham archdiocese, and so their absence sealed something in Margaret's resolve. This was where she was, and this life was spitting her out. She paused, cursorily, to consider how things might be different if she had stayed in the denomination she'd been born into, if David had been born in it too. They could marry; they probably would, in order to work as a team. They would be one clerical self, and each of them would work to their strengths. She was good at talking to women. He was kind. He was glamorous.

These things could not be underestimated.

She stopped herself in the thought and sewed the pinned pieces together one by one.

To think these things was to betray the denomination to which she did belong, which she had chosen, as an adult, fully fledged in her faculties. The Church of England was careerist, in its current age little more than a form of civil service. In its origins, it was a sordid fix for a petulant perpetual boy of a king. What was happening now with the Second Council was a collective effort; a great sifting of the Church's central truths from the adaptable facts of successive centuries. The matter of female clergy, and clerical celibacy, were examples of the latter. The Catholic Church had changed, and would change. It could, and would, rouse itself to meet the new millennium. Margaret still wanted, so very much, to believe this. But there were other things she wanted more. She would not allow herself, just yet, to think these into being.

The blades of her scissors are closing over the excess seam allowance now, giving their clean croak and squeak. There are only the sounds of these tools, and the cloth as she shakes it out, spreads it over her lap, bends over it with the crescent blade of the stitch picker, cleaves the furrow she has just made in error. She is now as Berthe Morisot might have painted her: a woman sitting in some mediated light, engaged in some small labour, absorbed by the mind moving in her hands.

30

David rang to tell her he'd been invited to a conference. In Nottingham, he said. Sitting on the stool in the post room, Margaret uncrossed and recrossed her legs. – Oh yes?

– It's all a bit cloak and dagger. I'd need to drive up very early in the morning. The Grail are organizing it.

The Grail was an organization of progressive Catholic laywomen.

There was another long pause, in which Margaret could feel him weighing the question against the back of his throat. She dared him to say it without her help.

– Would you like to come with me? There will be plenty of people – women – like you.

And then:

– And I would benefit greatly from your edits. On my lecture.

Early on Wednesday, David stood in a working men's club and spoke of the need for worker priests – married, and living fully within the communities they served. The room was full; outside it was raining and inside, macs and umbrellas and woollens exuded their warm, wet smells.

Margaret sat in a middle row and caught David's eye often. When she did, she felt the light flood into her face, spilling into a smile.

– The priest is not called to be a professional full-time Christian, paid to perform the Christian works on behalf of others. David's hands held the lectern gently. His posture was easeful, gracious. – It is a Christian obligation, not a specifically priestly one, to instruct the ignorant, feed the hungry, visit the sick, the widows and the imprisoned, console the dying and the mourner. The more the priest is used for these roles (as a Christian he will do some of them of his own volition), the more others can think themselves relieved of the sweet yoke of Christian life.

He spoke softly, compared to when he was in church, and Margaret felt the ears of the room pitch forward to attention.

– The full-time 'pastoral' priest engaged in these activities is in grave danger of corrupting his flock by the very exercise of good works: his zeal may be commended but his saintly example is not copied.

They are at the slim cusp of a great many changes. The times are sliding now towards them at the far end of their decade. If they had met even three years later, all this would have been easier, the ways suddenly opened, so much less exile and shame. But they are not to know this. The modern, more compassionate ways, the great exodus from the religious life, are not yet known or imaginable to them.

Afterwards many men came up to David and shook his hand enthusiastically. They stood under the low ceiling of the bar and paired off to talk, looking out into the room over the rims of their pints.

One approached Margaret. It took her a moment to recognize him, then she realized with a jolt that it was Mack. He was wearing a red shirt with a blue tie. He watched her absorb this and smiled at her.

– Yes, I left the priesthood a couple of months ago, he said. It was a hard shove, but I was grateful for it in the end.

– What are you doing now? Margaret took a sip of her desultory white wine.

– I'm working at Ipswich Museum. A different kind of relic worship. He laughed: ruefully, with a touch of sadness.

– Long way from here, no?

– Well, that was by design. Then Mack shifted his posture slightly. – Do you know, Margaret, what happens when a priest leaves the priesthood? She could see him looking back into the room, to which she had her back turned.

– Yes.

– Are you sure? His eyes have alighted on something behind her. She turned to see David, talking to two other men and making them laugh. Margaret breathed in.

– Go on. Tell me then.

– Well, Mack began. The law of the Church does not distinguish between an affair between two adults, and interfering with children. They are the same crime. For him to do . . . *that* with you would be a *crime*. Carnal sacrilege. A desecration of the priesthood, and our vocation. He would be defrocked. Stripped of his standing. Cast out. He will not be allowed any contact with any of his former colleagues. He will not be able to return to any place where he was known as a priest. People define this in different ways. It might be the parish, it might be the diocese, it could be the whole country. But it most certainly includes where all his family live. There will be no support for him, psychological or otherwise. It would get into the papers. It would break his mother's heart, I presume. He will be a middle-aged man with no qualifications. He would not be able to talk about what he had been before. Therefore where would he live? How would he earn?

Margaret lowered her eyes into her glass.

31

1965

IN THE MONTHS which follow, there are more conferences. These take place inconspicuously in seaside towns and lesser places of education; the two of them travel together. It involves increasingly strenuous night driving, David slipping through the net of the parish schedule, Margaret ducking out through the post room after teaching, to catch the bus and meet David in town. When Sister Augusta asks her where she's going, she claims to have met someone. – That will do you some good, she says, her mouth tight. A woman your age should be long married by now.

Margaret and David speak for hours in the car about the direction to take his papers in. He experiences the proximity of their thighs to one another as a heat. He grows enamoured of her handwriting, the way it comes to him tracking all over the typed pages of his talks.

By that early summer of 1965, the optimistic mood of the earlier Council was souring. Even the most hopeful observers could see the hierarchy reasserting itself, the docket of debatable issues emptying. The discussions of clerical celibacy and female clergy had been blocked at a certain level. The changes offered instead included Mass in the vernacular, and the priest to face the congregation rather than turn his back to it. These were cosmetic at best. Bones thrown. All this lent a greater sense of urgency to the gatherings of priests and committed laypeople which Margaret and David had become a part of. They knew they were approaching a slope in the discussion, a sudden turn: a crackdown from on high, their talk labelled as seditious; or the sealing of another fate, the departure of people from the faith in their droves, irreparably. They were all aware that they were becoming more desperate, obvious. The threat of reprisals ran through their talk like a cheese wire, and they knew that it was only a matter of time before some among them took the fall for the rest.

And in another, a lesser Cambridge college this time:
— It was Christians, not papalists, who did away with slavery, and castrati, and got women half-emancipated; they are still not fully emancipated in Church, not in Rome. It was other Christians who got the idea of the welfare state, who do something about racialism, or world hunger.
— A major obstacle to the proper, what we can safely call the *lay revolution* is, clearly, the clergy, and in particular, I think, the celibacy of the clergy.
Margaret sat in the front row and felt her whole body blush.

— Some Romans, David said, in another minor function room or lecture hall of a redbrick university, its carpet worn and panelling scuffed, have questioned the authority of common theological opinions and historical forms of speech, and have dared to explain things better than St Thomas did.

All this happens outside the Roman Communion, and is regarded as a sign of life, a sign of the times, a sign of the Holy Spirit at work; but inside, this is a crisis of authority. A crisis for authorities who have overreached themselves, and a crisis of conscience for Catholics who refuse to be cabbages, paternalistically indoctrinated.

He was as magnanimous in his charms as a movie star made according to the old moulds. In the bars afterwards, she stood back and observed the generosity of his gestures as he was congratulated on the points he made. Other men loved him, she could see, saw his easy grace and unaffected cool. It came with a kind of vanity, an enjoyment of all eyes being on him, a pleasure in holding the room with his voice and his High Renaissance hands. But it was a vanity which compelled and implicated her, for at some point he always beckoned her over to where he stood, thronged by others, and introduced her. This is my Miss Bendelow, he would say. We write together. And she felt for a brief, bright instant, to be folded into the currency of his beauty, his wit, and to live in it, shining.

They ventured another lunch with Ralph and Anna. Their eldest daughter, Emma, complimented Margaret on her clothes. Margaret told her how she'd made them, and promised to show her. Ralph watched as Margaret sustained an entire conversation with James about the Civil War, which he was studying at school.

Alone in the kitchen, Anna pulled at her elbow.

– I know what you're doing.

Margaret tensed. The intonation gave nothing away.

– With the women.

Margaret held her breath and looked her in the eye.

– And I want you to know I think it is a very great thing. Anna was gripping her arm, hard. The last two children, you know. I did not want them. I thought my, my parts, would . . . come away. She motioned over her lower abdomen.

Margaret pulled the question into her mouth. – Do you still believe?

– I will believe until the end of my days. She smiled. – And I believe in David. I believe in you. I believe in my friends who are doing their best to raise their children. Marriage is my vocation and I am glad of it. But the Church is losing them. The young. I will not blame my children if they choose to leave.

32

ALL THAT SUMMER, they travelled together. They stayed in separate rooms in provincial hotels. Sometimes, once they returned from the conferences, there would be weddings winding down in the function rooms of these hotels, their doors flung open to parched grass, and Margaret and David would join in discreetly, dancing on the brown carpets patterned with saffron-coloured motifs, moving close and feeling the pulse in one another's wrists. He loved to dance with her. In that small interlude, before his life fell about him like bricks, it was one of his most profound pleasures. He had had so little opportunity to dance before, although he was good at it. His mother had taught him and his brother, when they were young, before the things which took them away from her, before school, the war, before he resolved to walk through the proscenium into this life. Margaret's back was subtly muscular. He came into this knowledge quietly.

There are many different ways to have an affair.

Smoking together in the dark. A golf course spooling below the terrace where they sit.

– You have a shutness about you, he said.

Margaret gives her cigarette an irritated drag. She did not think it would be so irksome, to be got the measure of like this.

She moved past his shoulder and the suggestion of her touch was like a flare falling slowly through the dark. Previously unlit parts of him, deep inside the barrow of his body, shivered.

All her life, people had tried to make her feel ashamed, had called her pretentious, affected, too clever. This had confused her, indeed, made her feel ashamed. And here was someone who met her there, parry to parry. Talk with David was a wide expanse of green, and her mind the bright bolt of chestnut-coloured horse upon it: fully extended, free.

Parting ways for the night in a hotel corridor. She unlocked her door, then leant against it. The plausible deniability of being two drinks in.

– David?

He turns from unlocking his own door. – Yes?

– You can come into my room. If you like.

She sees his answer in his back before she sees it in his face. Things lock. Bolts slide home.

She has torn it all down.

His eyes when he levels them at hers are full of hurt.

– You cannot ask that of me. Please.

She makes to brush it off.

– No! His anger startles her. – You can't do that either. You know, Margaret. You *know*. I can't. I have given up – my family – my standing. The things which would happen to me. I would be thrown – it is all I have. You can't. You cannot. Please. No.

She sees that he is shaking. He backs into his room.

The next day they rise early and drive back together. They do not speak, but make noises of reaction to the news on the radio. Nearing Stoke again he pulls into a lay-by and cuts the engine. They sit together looking in the same direction.

Margaret begins to say she is sorry.

– Margaret, please. David holds up a quieting hand. – We both know you cannot ask that of me.

– I know. I'm sorry. I just—He smooths his hands round the steering wheel, up, then down. Margaret has her hands thrust deep into her coat pockets, her whole body braced.

– What if you choose to go?

He gives a stunned slow swing of the head.

– What do you mean?

– Choose another life.

– There is no other life. I was called to this.

– David.

He hates and resents, suddenly, the feel of his name in her mouth. It is too familiar. He feels it as a form of touch from which he must move away.

– David. I don't know how much more of this I can take. The Council. The Church. Less and less of it is credible to me. Not the central tenets, but there is too much – *around* it all, too many poor interpretations by too narrow a group of people.

Then she says (and he will always remember the wren weaving in the blackthorn before them):

– I want to live in my body. With you.

– I wouldn't know how.

– You would. We would work it out. I would not make you feel ashamed. I promise.

He closes his eyes.

– I can't. Please. Stop. *Please*, Margaret. He bends his gaze to his signet ring and works it up and down his knuckle.

– But I want you.

– Please don't say things like that.

– It's the truth.

– I don't want it.

– I think we could do a good job of loving one another.

There is a long pause in which he frowns.

– That's not the kind of declaration I would leave all this over. Isn't it supposed to be different? Like the road to Damascus. Knowledge.

– No. Love is not like that. It's like driving in the dark. You do your best to the limit of your sight.

– How do you know?

– I probably don't.

– So what are you saying then?

– I am saying that I want to dedicate myself to the task of giving you your rest and pleasure.

– Pleasure is a paltry impetus.

– That is where you're wrong, I'm afraid.

– Why is this not enough for you?

– Because I want to know you in the other way.

– Why?

She shrugs. She wants to see him in his sleep. She wants to see the things which clothe him, lifted, so she may see him and all the ordered facts of him. She wants to breathe with him. She wants him to slip asleep in her arms. She wants him to lie inside her.

– I want a private life with you.

He swings the key back into the ignition. They drive on.

33

– When I was first invited to this conference, the idea was that I should talk to you on what it is like to be a lay Christian within the godless society. But then I was very generously and courageously given freedom to say what I most wanted to say, and that is going to be different, because I don't really live within the godless society, at least not right in it.

Margaret had been invited to speak. They were known, by now, as a unit, so although they had not spoken much since that week in June, he had agreed to drive her there, and sit in the projectionist's booth to do the slideshow. On the way, they had sat in silence. It was now July. There was one week left of the summer term.

– I lecture in divinity in a Catholic College of two to three hundred Catholics, pious and nominal and all the gradations in between. I find myself more or less in a halfway house because of my job.

She had, he noticed for the first time, a habit of rocking back and forth on the balls of her feet, which gave her the slight air of levitating.

– Little of what I'm going to say to you normally gets said openly. The majority of laypeople for obvious reasons do not know much of it. Too much lay involvement is not desired. And the clergy do not openly say what I am going to say either – for fear of reprisals.

A frond of honey-coloured hair came loose and she tucked it back in one mellifluous gesture. Her hands moved like wheeling birds, he could do no more than stand and look from afar. She was now shifting her weight from one leg to the other like an athlete, or an acrobat.

– Although I doubt any bishop would want to unfrock me.

Laughter lapped through the room, curling like bright saltwater through its many seats. She held their attention like a moon.

Behind and above them all, he clicked her slides into place on the screen over her shoulder. A detail from the Prayer Book of Bonne of Luxembourg came through, of Christ's side wound; she was saying the words, 'Time and time again, we see this distinctly vaginal imagery, and we already speak of the Passion *giving birth* to the Church.' He smiled at her pun even as it sent a frisson along his forearms.

Under the split beam of the projector, he knew she could not see him. He did as he could; looking at her with immunity. He looked at the shadows cast by her ears. Her hair. The way it hit back at the light. He studied her reading frown, and how she turned her face up at intervals, her gaze vague and generous, her small smiles to herself when she landed on a witticism of which she was proud. Her pleasure was palpable, and his enjoyment fell into step with hers.

In the lay-by that day, he had felt sorrow. Sorrow and panic. Sorrow: because she had laid herself at his feet like that, and he could not, despite his best efforts of will, imagine being so open, so very *porous*, with another. Panic:

because he felt the eyes closing in on him from everywhere. Not least his own.

But standing there in the dark watching her, he felt quicken inside him, consciously for the first time, the thought that he should like to wake beside a mind like that each morning. To stir in sun-shutter-slattered sheets, bring coffee; cook eggs. And for the first time, he allowed himself to follow the thought through: what must he do, what must happen to him, in order for that to be the way of things? And was he prepared to go through it all?

She was talking now of individual words and phrases in Hebrew, now in Ancient Greek, on the pronouns used for the Holy Spirit in the Septuagint (female).

– Why for instance, do we call Mary 'mother undefiled mother inviolate', unless we think everyone else who becomes a mother is in the process defiled and raped?

Her thoughts were falling out of her in perfect somersaults and swallow dives, her jokes landing like trapeze artists. She gripped the lectern lightly. She was so fully bodied, her mind coursing through her like pure water, it flowed and carved through them all. It was righteous, diluvian, sustaining. It swept them up and carried the audience with it, they were rafters at its mercy and must ride out the dips and plunge pools and coursing rapids, and trust that she would carry them to places new.

And she does. She speaks of the Gnostic Gospels, of Mary Magdalene. She quotes John Donne, Thomas Paine, George Herbert. She makes them laugh, great peals of pleasure and surprise at how she vaults from one thing to another, drawing new maps as she goes. In another world, she could have been the scholar who rose to stardom, with her charisma at the lectern, she could have slotted into the circuit of the travelling lecturer; they both could.

He pictures, briefly: tenure together in the imitative cloisters of some university on the east coast of the United States, the famous falls and turning of the leaves. But he knows also that now, under present circumstances, they, she in particular, would be thwarted at every turn. The world was on the ledge of itself and they are a few years too soon. Instead they will have to run. The heft of this thought settles over him like a cloak. They will have to run to a new place. A place far away from all those they know. And there they will lead a quiet life, not wanting to attract attention to their histories.

– Why does the Roman Church have to rule her people, the people of God, by fear and repression? One student of mine told me that her student friends in other non-Roman Catholic colleges said to her, 'Your Church is just like Soviet Russia, sending people to Siberia.'

The road which lies ahead will be lonely. But, he thought with a new self-assurance he felt himself to be borrowing, at that very moment, from her: it matters not how strait the gate. How charged with punishments the scroll.

I am the master of my fate. I am the captain of my soul.

No, he thought. We are not masters of our fate. We cannot be. But captains of our souls. That we can attempt.

All his life, he has been taught to yearn for eternity. Yet here is this singular brilliance, consigned to a small span of years. He places the two side by side in the scales.

He sits in the booth.

He thinks now of love and its metaphors of burning, blazing, flame. He does not find this to be true. She is all water for him. She has cleansed and quenched him, she made the desert bloom. She has gone down into the caverns of the holy writ, the chambers where iteration upon iteration of men have chipped away upon the walls in the dark, guided by the sounds of their own voices and the music their chisels make together. She has gone down to where they would not go, to where they had dug and dug no further because of the unruly mysteries they'd found. She went down into the deepest caverns where the waters waited, still and smooth and perfectly acoustic, and she had summoned them to surge. He has missed this, and many other things besides, in their time apart: her sigh of satisfaction at the sound of ice cubes cracking, her delight in a perfect green bean. The muscles at the base of her back. Her vicious wit. The confounding clarity of her convictions.

Will these things be enough?

He sits in the booth. He hears her voice, saying the Holy Spirit is female and always has been. He hears a voice inside his head say *you must marry this woman*.

Margaret lifts her eyes to where she knows he stands behind the rainbow beam. She knows he's looking at her.

– Of course this involvement of the priest in the world would be incomplete unless he were given the liberty to decide for himself, freely and responsibly – before God – whether he, as this particular individual, could best fulfil his ministry in celibacy – lifelong or for a limited period – or from within the companionship and commitment of marriage and parenthood. As the world is increasingly given to women, then the Church has no right to preach to the world a gospel which declares that in Christ there is neither male nor female. Women should be permitted to enter the clergy, in their numbers and in full. Almost all the other churches will ditch this antiquated thinking before we do. Our Church is not making new Christians, and this is one of the reasons why.

Each of them, David and Margaret, within the strictures of their own sight, imagined they had seen the other looking back, and held the thought for a moment as a small, precious thing.

They will be able to stop a room in its tracks with their perfect foxtrot, they will live in a number of countries where he does not speak the language, when he is carving a chicken he will relish asking, 'Leg or tit?', they will throw good parties and when he wears black tie she won't be able to keep her hands off him, he will grow a number of gardens and she will kill them all through neglect, and then will not apologize, they will never go back to live in England. He will find rest, of a kind, in a hot country, under the shade of a mulberry tree. He will eat olives there, and swim in the river, and walk a dog over the knuckled hills. They will come to know one another in a way that feels appropriate. He will never quite be able to give her what she needs, in bed. The knowledge of this, unshakeable, will well up inside him, hot like shame. It will lurk in his joints like inflammation. He will know that sometimes, in the night, she will get up to cry about this fact in the dark house. The orgasms, by and large, will abandon her. And they will never come back. He will always be shy about touching her. He will want to give it all to her, whatever it is, but will feel incapable. There will be a few occasions of sex which are pure transcendence: above the mind, pleasure like the vast starriness of space.

He will teach their child many practical things: how to mulch a rose and build a fire, how to drill pilot holes and make a bookcase. She will adore him. All this time is coming now, unspooling from the present: it is the goldfinch held in the hand, about to unfold itself and launch; it is the pomegranate spilling its red jewels from a small aperture in its side, it is the crags of the apple, after the bite. And he is held within it, a bubble in the honey, a reed in the stream, an insect in the amber.

He will feel lonely in his marriage now and again, and will know that she does too.

They will stand in Avignon, in the palace of the popes, and hold hands beneath the barrel vaulting of the great hall. At Sénanque she will rummage in the boot of the car for a shawl, a scarf, anything, with which to cover her shoulders under the eyes of the monks – she will be wearing a button-down sundress which now and again exposes her freckled legs. They will pick fresh figs off the trees in the liminal seams of the arable land. What is a marriage, if not the continued co-authoring of habits, good and bad?

34

2019

Let the majesty of it pass through you. Say the words.

They had to dress her in onesies which did up at the back now, because she'd got into the habit of ripping off her clothes and tearing into her nappy. Carers would come into her room and find her sitting on her bed, naked, smeared all over in her own shit.

Clothes had been almost comically important once. Which ones you put on, which ones you took off. Who was wearing what and what it meant.

She remembered now, one of those first times, how he had come into her arms. She felt like a student again, though she was nearing forty, in that almost comically strait single bed. Whose bed? What time of day or night? She had tried to do her usual thing of hiding her face in her hands, and he made a noise of objection and pulled them away, in order to look at her – some plea in his eyes – and it had bolted out of her.

He would come seeking her in his sleep, to hide his face in the crooks of her. She had known the private places of that man. She had sifted and withheld these facts from the years.

When she had been pregnant he left his hands on her all night long, and the creature nudged against his palm. Even when the years had worn them smooth with one another, he pushed as if he was trying to climb inside her.

The very first time he had touched her had been her hair. They were drinking in his new, his second, sitting room. Late. He had been praising her and her lecture, a detail therein which had delighted him; it had necessitated standing up, now he sat down heavily on the sofa, next to her. Too close. Plausibly an accident. The ice in their third or fourth drink clinked in their glasses. Her hair pinned low at her nape. His hand was on it, his thumb was smoothing over it. They were both very still while he did it. She drank from her drink and stared straight ahead but her scalp was singing with it. He found the pins which held her bun and pulled them out. He undid it. She felt it fall. He slid his hand inside her hair, feeling for the back of her head. She leant back into it. Her eyes closed. She said mmmm. His hand moved away quickly.

He had kissed her clumsily in his kitchen first. Yes. She had known that. His Adam's apple rising and falling just underneath the collar. She was sitting on the counter, swinging her legs at him. He walked up to her. Patted her knees to part them. Stood between them. Put his arms around her. There was a question in this. To which she said yes with the whole arc of her back.

The first time. Yes. He had eased the collar off the stud and left it on the desk. She remembered buttons, and the sound of his belt pulling back through the buckle, its soft fall to the floor. When she put the palm of her hand just beneath his navel – the beautiful staggering lip of it (that day at the beach) – and made it flush with the curve of his stomach, her fingers dipping beneath the waistband of his boxers (the hair began), he started to shake. She sat down on the bed, and showed him how to undo her garter. He knelt at the foot of the bed and held her feet in his hands. He smoothed his thumb over the bones of her ankles.

– Can you take this off, please? Gesturing at her skirt. She stood up and stepped out of it. His fingers frowning on the buttons of her blouse. She undid the clasp of her bra and dipped her arms out of its straps. The cups of it came away from her chest. She saw the change in his face.

Then: the pitch of her hips against his. The polite initial nudge of his penis against her uppermost innermost thigh. I'm sorry. I don't – know. Should I? Move your
    like this   not quite   that's it   I'm sorry
    don't apologize   is this?   what should I do?   try
He held her face in his hands. She felt for the tendons in his wrist with her mouth. The gentle pressure of his thumb on her lower front teeth. She didn't know what kinds of sound she made. The wide-eyed look he gave her when it was over.

Smells that she adored: thyme, that scraggled out of life in the garrigue; rosemary, cypress and bay in the hot concertos of the afternoons; cistus, fig skin; the limestone dust of the roads as it rose; the damp stones of Paris; the exhalations of pine needles when you stepped on them, your feet still tender from sandals you were breaking in; seaweed dying in the sun and its crackle; the shade of a church porch when first you stepped into it, parched.

The day the blood did not come on cue. It was that morning of rage and the miniskirt.

Our work is the unfolding of souls. Never forget.

A soul so enfolded was hard to open. She had tried her best.

She pictured a young man in his prime climbing into a fig tree's spread branches, throwing down green fruit which exhaled its ash smell of shade. The reach of the man in the tree. His waist like water cooling. My love, she thought, weighing the words in her mouth, *c'est toi l'amour de ma vie*. The gorgeous impossible hymn of the whole of him.

Her husband's mind thinning on the morphine. His mysteries marbling like paper. There was still such an abundance of things to talk about with him. How to tell a planet from a star. The lion metaphors in the *Odyssey*. Plants related to roses and their maintenance. John Paul II, Tibet, the G8 protests which were at that very moment unfolding in Genoa.
  – His pain threshold is so high, the district nurse said, the needle held aloft elegantly, like a cigarette she was about to ash, *c'est dangereux*.
  The body of her husband, monumental and out of time.
  The nurses came to do the injections, moving him onto his side to ease the needle into his back, where the dose was

written on a gauze patch. She saw the number rising by the day. The nurse's eyes meeting hers over his tan shoulder. Too tan, as it happened. Bad tan. These grey-eyed women who toured the area, administering dignity to the dying. They drove small white Peugeots in crisp short-sleeved shirts, their arms thin and freckled. Their cool assessing looks. They grasped the situation quickly, and squeezed her arm.

The morphine gave him hallucinatory dreams. The first time it happened, he kicked off the sheets and ran down the stairs to the heavy braced front door, had yanked it open and dashed out into the street, looking to the sky, shouting, *They're coming!* He slept naked, had done so all his life. The hands on the tower of the clock said two. She could not read him. Until. He held his arms up in exaltation.

– Who is coming to get you?
– The angels!
He grinned at her.

It was the same every night. Post and lintel of her life, undoing himself.

She had had to teach the man she married to touch her.

Sex is a series of constituent acts. The powers that be of the Second Vatican Council all seemed to agree on its irrevocable and definite endpoint, but its beginnings were harder to define. When does sex begin between two people? When they pass one another in a corridor, and all the pores of their arms catch the passage of the other, and hum? The first time the hand of one meets the surface of the other? When the body bucks, involuntarily? When does it become inevitable? Kiss me, he'd asked her, and then he came in.

35

Adrian used the first of his annual leave from his new job to visit from London. She was held into her wheelchair with a harness. In her room her bed was winched to its lowest possible height, and on the ground beside it there was another mattress. She had started rolling out of bed. There were dark bruises on her hands and shins. She tries to get up, the carers told him, and they put a hand on his shoulder. He wheeled her out onto the balcony and brushed her hair.

She said: 'I don't know where I am in the history of life. It's all very strange.' 'I don't know who I am'. He told her where she was.

– Do you remember?

– I think so.

– It was a beautiful cycle today. Do you remember how the light gets here, in the evenings, all gold in the trees?

                                         No.

– Do you remember Gung? Do you remember meeting him?

   – I can't talk

                            about this with you.

            My mind is too

                                muddled today.

There is a long pause. He watches her eyes roll around the room.

— Did you know, I met an Irish nun once. This was much later . . . after. She was headmistress at a girls' school near Cork. I asked her what they did when their girls got pregnant. And she said, 'What do you think we do, Sister? We get them over to England, quick as we can.' They needed chaperones, so I did that. For a number of years. When I could. Outside term time.

Adrian looks at her. She looks out of the window.

— I don't want you to think we made the decision lightly. We didn't. We considered it

                                                              very seriously.

— It became a matter, you see, of whether or not we were going to let it spoil our lives. At a given point you have to decide: am I going to let this spoil my life, or am I going to live? Well, we chose life. That is what you must do too, you know. Passion is only one mode of love.

— What do you mean?

— You know, passion. Capital P.

(She opens her arms like an albatross.)

— The naked man   espaliered there

— You mean Jesus?

                                  — Mmmhmm.

Then she says:

                                        — now wait a minute

At this he could scream.

What has he learnt here, at this time of his life?
    The olive trees look good in every light.
    Love is at its base the effort of dignity.
    Catch at every pleasure as it passes.
    There is no other place.

He goes back to her house and notices woodworm in what was her desk. So he pulls out the drawers and tips their contents out so that he can treat it. Receipts, bills for the old dogs' home she had supported, rubber bands, old chequebooks, an address book with many names now crossed out, and then the thing which calls itself a parable: some sheets of typewritten paper. In the top-left corner, a rusted rut where a paperclip has left its mark. While he reads it in growing disbelief, the Red Hot Chili Peppers play from a speaker in another room.

36

Parable

One quiet evening, a man discloses to his friends that he wishes, when he gets to heaven (he hopes), to conduct the celestial symphony orchestra.

In order to practise, the man chooses to be a conductor here on earth. The managers of the orchestra tell him he will be a better conductor if he has no instrument of his own. Instead he will direct others: he will read books. His own hands are not to take up the viola or the flute, the violin or the double bass, though he might occasionally bang a drum or clash the cymbals, strictly for recreational purposes.

The grand composer, who wrote the score for the celestial symphony, was said to be deeply concerned over every player on earth, though none of them had seen him in a very long time, and neither had the managers or the conductor. Many of the players, if ever they were in doubt that he was real, would turn to the conductor for reassurance, because they believed that he, and the managers, had private telephone conversations with him that they did not enjoy. The managers were pleased to foster this belief.

Then one day the conductor discovered that he dearly desired to play a duet with one of the players. To this end, he wished to take up the cello. Together they played some exquisite strains in a minor key, but because of his promise not to actually join in with the orchestra, they never let their music round out into the major, developed harmonies.

The managers caught the strains of the music the pair made together but, being in no ways musicians themselves, mistook it for cacophony. Then the duet player's instrument snapped in her hands, and none could mend it for her. She came to the conductor and said, 'I have been examining this score; it may look all right on paper, but I've been trying to play it, even before my instrument broke, and so have many others, and it comes out in harsh discords; either this is what the composer meant, or He is no true musician. We have tried ourselves to telephone Him, to write to Him, to get a message through to Him, since you have always told us that He cares about the music and the players, but we get no answer. Some among us are beginning to say He is not real, or that He does not care for His orchestra nor for our playing.'

Part of the conductor's job was to tell the orchestra that the true music could only be played if everyone heeded the composer's directives and the managers' directives as well – these especially.

So, the conductor would gather the players to explain the score to them, but he never wanted to hear their questionings, for he had no answers. And so, more and more left the orchestra, and gave up playing altogether. And, it should be said, all conductors all over the world were having these sorts of problems with their orchestras. To his fellow duettist he could only say: 'The most important thing of all is for us conductors to go on standing on the rostrum and conduct.

After all, there stands the concert hall, and the acoustics are splendid, there are all the instruments and lots of people have bought tickets, season tickets and even life-subscriptions ... the show must go on. Besides, I can't abide the idea that the composer isn't real or isn't interested in us, or that the score may be wrong. It must be right. And if it isn't, you see, I and all the other conductors would have to get down from our rostrums. Bent as my baton may be, the remaining members of the orchestra still obey it (and the managers do let us have programmes printed in English now). And if I lay down my baton, what else could I do, but take the tickets at the doors from the crowds coming in for the Beatles?'

37

1965

THEY WERE CAUGHT, of course.

Dwyer kept him standing this time. He glared at him, daring him to say it.

– I want to marry her. I would like to be released from my vows.

– We'll get to that, Fletcher. But a parable? Really? To stand up and say these things, in public? At the *pulpit*? It is a violation of your office. Not to mention *her*. Lecturing.

It was Monday. He and Margaret had returned from her talk on Saturday. He had stayed up into the early hours writing the parable, and delivered it on Sunday. It had had a mixed response from the congregation. Muted laughter at mention of the Beatles.

Dwyer told him he was weak, disgusting, feeble, had committed carnal sacrilege. He spat the words *bluestocking* and *bit of skirt* at him with contempt.

Well, which is she? David thought to himself. And then: she is both. Which is why I never really stood a chance. And so here we are.

– I have thought it over.

Dwyer licked his lips, then took his time telling David

what would happen. No one will speak to you, he said. None of my priests. Do not hope for help from us. And when she tires of you, you can't come back. He was leaning forward over his desk now, rocking back and forth with the force of his words. David saw the same erotic flash he had seen all those years ago, in the priest who lifted the whip at school. Droplets of Dwyer's spit landed on David's face, on the lenses of his glasses. David was still; he did not reach up to wipe them away. David did as he had been trained all his life to do: he stood and took it. Dwyer told him he would need to write the letter, explaining that one had been mistaken about one's calling, one had been unfit to be a priest all along, one was weak and corrupted, the most pathetic of sinners.

When it was over and he'd been excused, David called Ralph from a phone box and asked to borrow money for an engagement ring. Ralph said yes and asked no further questions. He invited him home for supper, and David went, and wept in his brother's arms. He had one month's pay.

Ralph was there when he told their mother the next morning. They worried she might be about to have a stroke.

– Was it for this?
– What do you mean, Mummy?
– What have you done?
– Nothing, Mummy. It is love. I am at its mercies.
– My darling. Go now, please. I cannot look at you. For now.

Margaret had been with David when he received the summons from Dwyer.

Of course the sisters knew too.

Sister Augusta summoned her into her office, called her a slut and slapped her.

Margaret let out then redid her hair.

– Are you finished?

She called Eileen, and then Anna, from the post room. An hour later Anna was waiting at the gate in the car. She helped Margaret carry the sewing machine down the drive. Once on the front seat, Margaret said *damn* and pressed her palms into her eyes. Anna reached for her hand, pulled her close, rubbed circles on her back.

– He loves you.

– We don't know that.

– Oh, but we do.

– What must you think of me?

Anna took her back to the house and made her lunch.

– I'm sorry that you can't stay with us.

– That's all right.

– Where will you go?

– I have a friend back in Sheffield who can put me up. For some time, if need be. I think.

– It may not come to that.

– I think— She is playing the tip of her finger along the tines of her fork. There are tears gathering at the bottoms of her eyes. – I am tired of having no home.

– Keep faith.

– It will all come to naught. Her voice cracked on 'naught' and she brought her hands up to her face, the words coming hard and fast as heaves now. – My leaving. No one will remember. It will all roll on indifferent.

– We shall see.

Anna drove her to New Street station. On the way they stopped by Dwyer's office.

She was wearing a miniskirt. She swore at him, told him the Old Mother Church was a bitch. Then she left, slamming the door, shutting him back into his life. She was the world, and he had not wanted it: the place in which he was left standing was oak-panelled and dark.

Later that week Ralph walked into Dwyer's office and said: May you burn in hell for what you have done to my brother.

38

STAFFORDSHIRE SENTINEL, THURSDAY, 30 July 1965

R.C. priest leaves Burslem parish

Father David Fletcher, aged 41, who until recently was the Roman Catholic priest at Burslem, has left because of health reasons and is staying with relatives, a spokesperson for the diocese told the Sentinel.

Father Fletcher has been parish priest at St Joseph's Roman Catholic Church, Burslem, since last November. Before moving to Burslem, he was parish priest at Monks Kirby, Warwickshire, from 1953 to 1964. He will take over another parish, it was stated, when his health improves sufficiently.

Father Fletcher left Burslem just over a week ago and his place has been taken by Father Oliver Hesketh, aged 38, who was assistant priest at Wednesbury, South Staffordshire. He arrived last Friday.

39

He proposed to her with a fruit bowl.

She was always eating fruit. In hindsight, this would seem like a bad joke – a ham-fisted reference from a rueful creator – but it was true: asking if he had any, or eyeing the greengages on his trees through the kitchen window back in Monks Kirby. He had let her strip them now and then, lent her a bucket or a basket for them. She spoke to him between mouthfuls of pear or peach. She picked the grapes from the vines along the garden wall absentmindedly, crunching their seeds. She didn't seem to be aware that she was doing it. He had a print of persimmons hanging in the hall, which he'd bought in Burma. What fruit is this? she asked him. They look like lanterns. When he explained about their hazard-orange flesh, flecked with tiny touches of brown like spice, her eyes widened.

He drove to Stafford and looked in the potters' windows for the biggest bowl he could find. The one he chose was wide and shallow, with a pattern of pink and purple pears. Then he bought a ring.

It would take him three years to pay Ralph back.

When the day came, he closed the door in the garden wall.

He handed her the bowl, wrapped in brown packing paper and tied with twine, and waited for her to unwrap it. When she had, she smiled her question at him. From behind his back he produced the ring, loose, closed in his hand. He opened it above the bowl and the ring dropped into it, where it made a minuscule musical sound.

She looked from it to him.

– For me? she said. For ever?

– Yes.

And then he said:

– I want to talk to you. For the rest of my days.

They grinned at each other then, and she put the bowl to one side so she could hold his face in her hands. He pulled her onto his lap and held her there, and she stroked his hair and let her lips rest at his temple, and they stayed like that together for a long time, until the light went glaucous and a chill crept into it.

David wrote to a friend who worked for the British Council and asked if he knew of any teaching jobs going. The friend replied: teaching adults English, in Tehran or Misratah, Libya.

They chose Misratah.

He rang around for where to have the wedding.

– I've made enquiries. Kensington will do it.

– All right.

They posted the banns through the council. He was staying with Ralph. She had called the woman who helped the runaway wives, and was staying in the attic of a widow's workers' cottage in Birmingham.

They spoke of the marriage vows laid out in the Book of Common Prayer, agreeing that this was the better version. It was an almost-perfect text, they agreed, mouthed and metabolized by the many. – With my body I thee worship, he said, under his breath.

– Whereas in the Catholic ceremony, the priest has the central role. He has the most lines, she chuckled.

His name was David. Lots of men were called that then. But still, it felt like a cosmic joke, a jab in the ribs. He was David, slinging his stones. Bernini's boy, biting his lip. She was just the woman, temptress. She thought of Susannah squirming away from the Elders. Their gaze and grasp. The dripped pearlescence on her thighs. Everywhere her form was there, but it was insubstantial, vague. She liked the iconography of Joseph most. Always that same kindness in his face.

She wanted to see his most secret faces. To live in the suchness of things, with no shame. Yes, she exhaled, that was the task which lay before them.

The night before they left for London, they went to dinner with Ralph and Anna. Partway through drinks, Anna led her upstairs by the hand. There were two rooms under the eaves, one for the boys and one for the girls. Margaret followed her into one of them. On one of the narrow beds was a Moses basket, and in it, clean stacks of cloth nappies, squares of muslin, crocheted blankets, tiny clothes.

– I don't need these things any more, said Anna. But you

might. She reached for Margaret's hand and squeezed it, hard. I am sorry you will be so far away.

The two couples – for Margaret and David were now, irrevocably, a couple – looked at one another over the vestiges of their meal. Ralph ran his fingertip round the rim of his glass of port.

– Be good to him.

Anna reached through the window on the passenger side as they pulled away from the drive. The basket was in the back. Ralph had put it there wordlessly, and David had not looked at Margaret as he did so. Anna gripped again for Margaret's hands. – Courage, she said.

David drove her back to the house where she was staying.

They had not really spoken about what was happening. It felt as if they were freighted for it, one event was succeeding another. Tomorrow they would stand in some minor carpeted room of a public building and sign paperwork and be married, and henceforth be alone.

– Goodnight, David, my love.

– Goodnight. The car door closes.

My love. He can feel the way she has rolled the words around her mouth like stones.

40

1965

THE PLAN, a quaint concession to superstition, was that David would drive the car, loaded now with all their possessions, down to London, and Margaret would travel alone on the train, with her one neat suitcase. They had an appointment at Kensington Registry Office for three o'clock that afternoon. She checked into the hotel where he had booked two separate rooms. She ran a hot bath and got into it. She got out of it and did her hair. She put on her new green silk suit. She did her face, she brushed her teeth. She walked out into the corridor, carpeted in lurid rose-coloured lozenges. She called the lift and stepped into it. It slowed as it came to the ground floor. The doors opened, feeling suddenly ancient, like something cut out of their original structure, the chamber of the king from a pyramid. She walked out into the hotel lobby, contracting the muscles of her ankles. And he was there, sitting in a tub chair, standing to greet her. He was wearing a suit – his civvies, the thought flashed before her mind – for the first time since she'd known him, a dip in his collar now to accommodate for his throat and at it, fastened, a red bow tie. With his new clothes she wavered a little like a taper in a draught. Would she know him? Was he the same? He saw it cross behind her eyes and rose with greater urgency, his hand coming out now to her arm. The pulse. The drumming.

He had in his pocket the ring, which he'd had engraved with the words *hic sunt leones*, the ancient Roman admonition which floated at the edgelands of maps: here be lions. They were moving into wild, unknown country. It would make strange beasts of them.

They caught the 328.

It happened in a small room, pastel blue. Sanded glass sconces lighting the room; an enormous picture of the Queen resting on an easel. A tepid bunch of hydrangeas in a vase. Some rows of empty fold-out chairs.

The questions were asked of them. Did they know that marriage was a contract between one man and one woman? (The registrar's speech falling like a mallet on *one man* and *one woman*.) They did. When they said their I dos it felt like a borrowed phrase.

David looked at the registrar and thought back to Ralph's wedding. This man would join them and then go back to an office, where presumably he rubber-stamped planning permissions, a paper pusher in a minor outpost of a sprawling bureaucracy.

Margaret held his hand. Had it all been different, had it been in a church, she would have walked alone down an aisle to meet him; or her parents, still alive, might stand in unison and say, 'She goes of her own free will' when the priest asked of a crowded room: 'Who brings this bride to be given away?' When it came to the ring she held her hand out, fingers artfully bent in a way that suggested no effort, like some beauty of the Quattrocento. They signed the register and she looked at her name. Her occupation had been entered as 'spinster'. The nib caught with a loud scratch.

At the end of it they walked back out into the black cab belch-and-fug of the King's Road. There was no one there to sting them with rice. She had no flowers and did not know what to do with her hands. He took one arm and linked it through his. They had the town hall photographer for fifteen minutes. They walked round to a small garden square and stood stiffly. Later, looking at the prints, they were surprised to see themselves grinning from ear to ear. They stood at the counter in the photo shop, pointing and laughing at themselves. He had his hand on the small of her back. She had been acutely aware of him putting it there, the soft, tentative way it had landed and then proceeded to move in feathered patterns. All the hairs on her arms had stood up so fast they began to sing against the silk of her shirt.

It was booming in them. In their chests and their ears and their necks. In their knees and their feet. Every hair on their heads tingled with it, with what was next. The cause for which they'd been ordained.

Margaret was thirty-eight. She'd done things in a high room in Rome with a lithe man younger than her, with handfuls of curls. She'd leant against bars appraisingly. She'd been beached by orgasms before, felt their starry sea-foam at dawn. She'd loved Tristan Andrews. She'd seen David almost naked, that day at the beach. She thought for a moment of the body she knew beneath his clothes: that taut middle, not like Michelangelo's *David*, but some torso of Apollo dredged up from the sea after a thousand years – soft in its hills and vales.

41

– Give me my sin again, she joked. Reaching for it.

They were in bed. In the first of a series of hotels and bed and breakfasts between Folkestone and Naples.

– I always preferred *Antony and Cleopatra*, you know. 'The odds is gone' and all that.

She did not.

– When did you read *Antony and Cleopatra*?

– When I lived alone.

They fetched his Arden Shakespeare from a suitcase and opened it over his thighs. She lay with her head on his chest, or in the fold of his shoulder, her fingers always finding some small thing to occupy themselves with on his body. All that talk of mud and ooze, she said. Are we like that? Am I the woman who stole you from Rome?

Lying uncovered in the late-night half-light, the pattern of their breath descending, she traced his bent knee. This is *so* beautiful, she said. He touched the same place on her, and said the same thing. It was the first time he'd ever let her look so long at him.

❖

Waiting to board the ferry in Dover, they had watched as a couple of a similar age let their dog cock its leg against the cliffs, and they had laughed together. They'd woken up in their hotel room, painted three different shades of cream, and he had reached for his trousers, slung over the back of a chair, and put them on while still in bed in order to get up to go to the toilet. She had made the mistake of laughing, and their shared mirth now was a fragile truce.

Their wedding night had been awkward, and over too quickly. She had always known that would be the case, but still, when it happened, it was hard to say it had been momentous. He hadn't known how to undress her, had been baffled and wrong-footed by the variety of different fastenings on her clothes. He had been completely silent all the way through.

Now stood on deck, they watched the surf smack against the sides of the boat. He went back down to the car and sat in it alone while she tried to read her book in the lounge. In the hold, the chains which held the lorries clinked.

Paris was a detour, but they went because it was where you were supposed to go on honeymoon. They stayed in a chambre de bonne near the Panthéon, and walked downhill to the Quartier Latin and across the river. They got sorbet at Berthillon and swapped cones halfway through, they linked arms. They queued to climb the towers of Notre-Dame, but it was a mistake. She was walking ahead of him, and it was only part of the way up, the spiral staircase barely as wide as their shoulders, no way to turn back through the long procession of tourists, that she turned to look at him and saw he was opening and closing his mouth silently, trying to say, she thought, her name. He was sweating. He collapsed into the narrow alcove of a window sideways, and there began to shake. The man behind him stopped abruptly and raised his eyebrows at Margaret. David was convulsing, his knuckles white on the rope banister, and his foot slipped from the step. The queue of people was bunching up now behind them. She lunged for David, her feet landing awkwardly on two different steps, and tried to catch him before he slid off the slope of the windowsill. She received almost the whole weight of him into her arms, and it forced them both to their knees. The man who'd been behind David caught her back and braced all three of them with an arm against the inner wall. Noises of concern were passed down the helix of the queue. David was sobbing into Margaret's shoulder, the heaving of his body moving into her muscles where she held him.

Now the couple who had been in front of Margaret had turned around and together all four of them managed to get David into a slumped position at the wide end of a step, leaning back against Margaret between her knees as she sat on the next step up, his fall blocked by those below, with a narrow impasse for others to move past. This they began to do, picking their way slowly past and nodding gravely or otherwise averting their eyes. Someone offered him a drink from a steel water bottle, and another broke off a square of chocolate for him. He was very pale. She held his head in her hands and bent to whisper in his ear.

– My love, she said, it's all right. She had never called him that in public. He wove his left arm under her leg and held it from beneath, turning his face into the inside of her knee. He was trying to slow his breathing. She stroked his hair, smoothed her hand over his back. An older couple moved past, and the woman reached out to touch Margaret's shoulder. David shifted backwards, tipping his head onto the crook of Margaret's arm. His eyes were closed and his shaking had slowed into prolonged shivers. She bent over him and kissed his temples, cupped his cheeks and jaw. She began to murmur St Francis's Canticle of the Sun into his ear. At this he tried to smile. Families filed past, speaking many languages.

Eventually David sighed and opened his eyes. They looked at one another and he felt for her hand. He brought it to his mouth and kissed her knuckle. – I'm so sorry, he said. She shook her head. – We can't turn back, she said. So they made their way to the top – not so far, in the event – escorted by the man who'd been behind them. They saw the bells on their wooden trusses but moved swiftly on, and crossed the gallery where the gargoyles pondered. They did not take in the view. They descended the other tower and walked back out into the sunshine on the other side. They crossed onto the Rive Droite and plunged into the medieval streets of the Marais, whence the cathedral could not be seen.

They found a perfectly average bistro and ate big, brassy salads and a glass each of some clear cool white wine. In their room later, with the lights off, he let her undress him, and in the morning, he woke her by stroking her hair. They checked out and bought croissants and ate them straight from the bags on the front seat, heading east off the périphérique.

After the sex, better than the sex, was the talking. He allowed himself to lie in her arms and they spoke of all the things upon which their minds alighted. Kissing like punctuation. Some part of the other under their hands. Moving their fingers idly. – Mmm, she said, more of that please (his hands on her back). Her fingers at his temples. Her lips at his ear. His head on her belly. They spoke of many things, their talk breaking off and resuming, rising and falling, sleep and sex.

They headed to Reims, Metz, then Saarbrücken, and on to Stuttgart and Munich. David kept a list of their expenses. *Ralph says he'll pay*, she saw him pencil beneath.

In Innsbruck she had eaten some vast, rich dish which made her sick.

Suspicions of a baby, she wrote in her diary.

Their brakes failed heading up the Brenner Pass. She tried not to read it as a sign. She was done with signs. There were none, or they meant nothing, or she was leaving them behind. Here on the saddle of this tiny, brash continent, where Hannibal had whipped the elephants up the steep inclines, she stood and looked out south with a hand coming down to rest, of its own accord, on the space below her ribs. She stood there on the ledge of things like Cassandra on the ramparts of Troy. *Ich kann nicht anders*. That thing she had called her faith which had raged here, and elsewhere, like so much deforesting flame; which had sent Constantine conquering. Each and every war fought in its name. All that damage done. All those souls curtailed. She renounced it all. The vast history of Catholicism was folding and unfolding all around her, and folding her into it. It was in the mineral memory of the land. When stripped down to its barest, it was the history of being, of evolving personhood, the notion thereof, and its validity. She stood for this. She stood for herself. She knew that her protest would be a small footnote in its onward march, ultimately. That had always been Catholicism's appeal: the sublimation of oneself to something so much larger, something ancient and unbroken, its acoustics ringing through you for life. Behind her, her husband spoke to the AA man on the hard shoulder. Here was this man she was tasked to love while ever they should both be living. She squared her shoulders.

They stayed in Verona.

She overhears him humming Prokofiev in the shower. She writes in her notebook about romantic love treated as its own agenda, a valid one: the first time is in the story of Tristan and Iseult, or Isolde, a romance found in the twelfth-century Breton.

While her husband soaps himself, Margaret stretches beneath the sheets.

– Romantic love is not enough. It never is. Romeo and Juliet were young, and their love never got old. That was its blessing.

They are walking in the street, beneath a hundred balconies trailing with roses and trumpet flowers and jasmine.

– But you are forgetting, David says, Antony and Cleopatra. They are older. And it's better.

He lays his arm around her shoulders and the confidence of the gesture catches her off-guard.

He is looser here, in Italy. He wears a linen shirt with the two top buttons undone, is easier in his movements. He has developed a laconic, leonine cool, as he orders drinks and olives in Italian, lowering his sunglasses. At night he is getting more and more at ease, too, his hands smoothing her sides with greater self-assuredness. I like this, he says, with her hips in his hands.

In Bologna they went to see a doctor, who confirmed her pregnancy.

Her first reaction was sharp, resonant dismay. It was too soon. She was almost forty. It wasn't supposed to be this easy. But then, she supposed concurrently, it always was, and that was the flaw in their design.

They took a detour to Monterchi, climbing the hill into town and stepping into the church. It was mid-afternoon. So hot. Margaret felt faint. She sat down heavily on a pew to catch her breath. There it was, in the cooling smell of the stone, *Madonna del Parto* by Pierro della Francesca. Margaret had only her nausea and a man's word for it that there was something beginning to stir inside her, but the Virgin before her was so resolutely human, weighty, straining under her load. Even her shoulders were bowed. Mary's dress let out and open over her belly, which was its own force in the fresco. Mary's hands were those of a real pregnant woman: using the bump to rest, finding their way to the poses of all pregnant women since time immemorial, the pelvis shifted forward, that dull downward drag in her face. Her weariness gathered in her jaw and her gaze was low and heavy-lidded. She was like a horse upright and asleep. To look at her was to look at a woman in two places at once: become a body of the upward air at the same time as she was being held fast to the earth by muscular forces not her own. Never before had Margaret seen a painting so sure of where its weight lay. Again she found herself letting her hand come to rest on her belly. She sat like that for a long time, sometimes standing up and stepping forward to look at the surface of the plaster at an angle.

Its texture fascinated her: it was like skin bearing shallow hollow scars, from smallpox perhaps. Outside, a sparrow skittered past on vermicelli legs.

The two halves of her life swung out on either side of her precipitously. She thought of her long-dead parents, so tender and mild; and of her friends from college now all ensconced with families of their own; and of Sister Frances, Sister Helena, Sister Marcella, their bright fresh faces and girlish grace. And the other half sloped down, to places she couldn't foresee. She had talked to Tristan about this image. A lifetime ago. There was the momentary shiver, through her body, of the life she might have lived with him. Was she living a love story? she wondered. Is this what it was supposed to feel like? She permitted herself, momentarily, to wonder: is this how it would have happened, had he been under different strictures, had he not been a priest? They wouldn't be leaving, she conceded. But would they be married? Would they be sleeping with each other? Maybe. It would never have been the shattering act that it was now. The whole thing could have been abandoned if it had been unsatisfactory to her. Instead she must now stay the course.

She looked for David in the half-light. He was outside, sitting on the steps. He had his head in his hands.

She went to him.

– Margaret. She pulled his hands away, and ran her fingers along the lines of his palms.

– Please love me. Please love me well.

– I do love you.

– Please. We have to do it properly.

– We'll try our best. We'll do it to each other. Together.

– We are all alone. His voice cracking.

— We're not alone. We have the little sprout.

And she brought his hand to her stomach. This little conjured creature, curling like smoke within the red walls of her. Finned and gilled. It had come unbidden, and too soon. She stood and looked at David, who was now her husband. She saw this man naked now, slept alongside him, lay her hands upon him.

The novelty of this will never wear off.

She was married and pregnant. She was going to do it after all. And it was to be the great stand of her life.

The next day, they drove without stopping to Naples. They stood at the back of the boat and watched themselves retreating from land and the furrows the ferry made on the water. The wind played with their hair and showed where David's had thinned.

When the gangplank was lowered onto the quay in Tripoli three days later, they'd been waiting in their car for over an hour, and the vibration in the belly of the boat had sent Margaret to sleep. She was lying with her head in his lap, and he had to operate the gearstick at an awkward angle in order to move off. As soon as they drove out into the light, the heat hit them. David had his arm around Margaret as they waited to get through Customs. They had befriended another English couple during the crossing, much younger, he in oil and she pink and pertly pregnant, on their way back from a visit home. They'd offered to guide Margaret and David through the city and out, onto Misratah, where they also lived. Once on the other side of Customs, David found them waiting for him in their Jeep. They had a water cistern in their car, and had filled up two bottles and passed them through the window to him. He slotted in behind them. – Stay close, said the husband. The driving here is something else.

In the event, he didn't find it all too different from the driving back in Rome. In the city centre, there were still signs in Italian, but as they drew further out, these were either dishevelled or disfigured, or missing altogether. David's hands were sweating on the steering wheel. Eventually they were out of the city completely – it ended quite abruptly, a last row of houses and then tufts of tenacious grass gripping argile-coloured ground. The road hugged the coastline and the sea was bright and glazing. They stopped at a scenic viewpoint and asked Melanie and George – those were their names – to take their picture on the beach, but it was too hot to linger there any longer. Out of the corner of his eye, David watched as Margaret rested her face on her hand, her elbow on the armrest, and looked out of the window. Occasionally she played with her wedding ring. Mostly she was silent. It was dark by the time they got to Misratah, and pulled up in front of the little house that his new British Council colleague had arranged for them: white, rectangular with rounded edges. The front garden consisted of a rockery and a crimson oleander. He thought he could smell the thick sweet of lemon blossom on the air. His colleague was waiting for them, leaning against a Range Rover, wearing white drawstring trousers and a loose, short-sleeved shirt. Hands were shaken, keys were proffered, swinging on a ring; there was a brief tour. Then they were left alone, their feet shuffling on tiles, fumbling for light switches in the dark. She made the bed while he undid the cords tying their luggage to the roof of the car, then brought it all in piece by piece. They had cold showers. They got into bed. He leant back against her chest, between her legs, and she rubbed his shoulders. He lay down in her arms.

42

1966

THE NIGHTS WERE hot. There were always the clang of metal doors and the howling gaunt cats which loped along the tops of walls, the cool noise of a neighbour's fountain. Sometimes fascist-era Italo pop could be heard in snatches further away. They again got used to the movement of their respective bodies under heavy linen sheets. The last time they had felt the cool grain against their naked calves had been years apart, in Rome; hot dry nights in narrow beds with bells apportioning the hours. They had been in ignorance of one another then. Here the muezzin sounded twice before dawn, a keening, long-line rhythm discernible in the language they could not understand.

This was how he saw it: they left their little cairns of touch on one another.

This was how she saw it: he kissed her cursorily and it starved her.

At night, she lay on her back in bed and let tears pool coolly in her ears. Now and again, and many years hence.

The truth was that when it came to sex, she unsettled him.

When she came to him, seeking it, or guided his hands in her touch, or nudged him nakedly, sleepily, in bed, he didn't know what to do. There was no muscle memory to draw on, and he felt his body was too old to be learning these things afresh.

It took a long time for the sight of her unclothed to stop provoking a sharp internal lurch of alarm. The first time that he discovered that she preferred to clean the bathroom naked, he was ashamed to have been startled into shouting. The parted door's clacked retreat. Her sponge stilled mid-air, bemused. He hated her bemusement. It made him shrink inwardly. Here was a place where the depths of his innocence slapped him hard across the face every time. As her belly grew, she cupped it from beneath, and he flinched at the felt privacy of the gesture.

She couldn't shake the sense that sex was something to which he was indifferent, even now, when it had been the hinge upon which his life had swung. And they had so little time in which to get it right. Every day the knot of the baby thickened inside her. He would know her body changing, then changed, a fact for which she did not feel quite ready.

The baby kicked for the first time. He had that sense again, as he'd had through the fabric of Anna's dress, of a cave wall, and something conjured, some spectre of an animal, moving up through the rock to the surface of the stone.

Her belly grew. Her back curved. When he rubbed it, passing by, she rocked back into his touch with a low moan. The veins of her breasts came forth in colour, like the rivers of the earliest maps.

As she got bigger, he became nervous about sex, but she

insisted. – It's all right, David. It's all right. You won't hurt us. Then she joked, and it didn't land: – We have to practise.

In the shower she sits on a stool. The domes of her runnel with the thin soapy opacity of quartz-coloured water. She intrigues him. – You look like the Hagia Sophia.

– Excuse you! She grins and it is like the beam of a lighthouse sweeping. She splashes his face. – Will you wash my hair?

While he stands there at the white rim of the shower's base, filling and pouring the jug, he looks at her lashes. – I feel I am being weighted onto the earth, she says. Then: – When you do this, I feel it in my feet. All the way along my back to the base of my spine. It spreads through the root of my brain. Thank you. Thank you, my love.

He soaps her feet and makes her laugh. He smooths his hand round the beginnings of the bump, runs his finger round the daily-raising bud of her navel. When she makes to stand, he offers her his hands and enfolds her in a towel; he leans back against the wall to watch her work her comb through her hair. They look at one another. There are lines engraved at the edges of their eyes.

Cheese like weathered stone. Olives wrinkled like palms. The cracking of ice cubes in a glass, the responding loosening at the small of his back. His wife in a sundress. His hand on her leg, up the dress. Her *Mmmmm*. The backs of her knees, where kisses made the sounds of fish leaping from a river, in the dawn and middle distance. The ghosts of her feet in her sandals, the smooth shallow vale left by her big toe. The nape of her neck, where the hair was no border but gradations of itself, soft then gathering, then a sonata. The sound of her hair slide undoing, the whisper you might catch of it all coming down. Her mouth pursed with pins. The bead curtain parted in the morning and the smell of coffee. Laundry flacking on the line. Her, holding a full, rotund jug; caught in the mirror: the water bearer, his slaker of thirsts.

    He finds himself, at the midpoint of his life, thrown inside a motif: the desert, a dry place of wandering and no water. And he finds it to be wrong. This land is a place of bright, tenacious life. You just have to be patient, and read the signs to look for it.

She loved the parts of him not often enumerated as most erotic in a man. The isthmus at the hip, where the veins run pigeon-coloured and kingly blue.

43

AND OF COURSE then the baby was born. It was not that things were never the same after that, it was that things never really had time to become the same. He looked back on his marriage before the birth of his daughter not as an idyll but as an interlude, a clutch of months in which he'd had to learn things quickly.

A few days before the due date, they'd planned to drive into Tripoli so as to avoid having to get to hospital when the labour had already started. The distance was not so long, as the crow flies, but the road was narrow – barely wide enough for a car to pass a lorry – and went through country which was prelude to the Sahara, dry and prone to sandstorms, constantly being encroached upon by the elements. The road had been laid by the Italians in a hurry, thirty or so years before, just a strip of tarmac laid down on the sparse gravel in a straight line. Consequently it was thin, chipped at its edges, with large potholes. Wherever possible, David tried to drive around these, but if he hit one, Margaret would groan, shifting her hips in the seat. It took several hours and they set off in the middle of the night, for the heat. Margaret slept next to him, her head on the seat by the gearstick. Her hair was in a long plait straight down her back and she wore a shift dress, white, patterned with small yellow daisies.

After a few hours they changed over. He pulled off the road into a gravel slipway and shook her shoulder gently. She sat up, passing a hand over her forehead. It was before dawn but the air had taken on the dusty quality of the very early morning, as if the particles of light had been caught in the process of coalescing. There was no sound, not a tree or a bird, the night-calls of no animals. To the east, in the direction they were headed, they could see a paler rim of blue at the horizon. There was no other light. In the car headlights they could see clutches of grass breaking through the sand at irregular intervals. He got out of the car and walked round to open her side. She shuffled towards him and he put both of his arms out. She grabbed him just below the elbows, their forearms matched now and gripping each other, and pulled. She let out a groan which was part-laugh. She walked around the car, moving from side to side like the needle on a dial, before sliding into the driver's seat sideways and reaching blindly for the lever. She did, and sent herself back with a jolt; she looked up at him – he'd followed her on her walk around the car anxiously, and now hovered over her. She giggled. She swung her legs in and guided her belly round until it was just touching the steering wheel. He watched her reach for the pedals with her feet. She was barefoot, her white leather sandals were in the footwell on the other side.

– OK, partner, she said. She smiled and her teeth were the most distinguishable thing for miles around. He bent to kiss her bare shoulder, smattered now with freckles. He walked back around the car and got in next to her.

They drove until the sun came up. As they approached the city, its sodium lights picked out against the thinning blue, they pulled over once more and swapped again. Some joke about it not being respectable for him to be seen being driven by his pregnant wife into town.

They were staying with strangers, Sicilians that their neighbours had put them in touch with, friends of theirs from their early days in the country. By the time they rolled into the old town it was getting hot, a cool morning breeze coming in off the sea and cutting through the climbing bake of the day. The city had several neat patterned lawns; circles made up of triangles of bright, improbable green. The buildings reminded her of Rome, and there was something in Mussolini's project to be seen in the facades composed of smooth arches and pastel-coloured stucco, and covered arcades where you could walk for miles without ever leaving the shade. There were few cars and they passed many men with donkeys on the ends of rope, laden with baskets containing branches of dates, or oranges. They found the building where they were staying. It was unfinished, steel girders still poking out of the roof. The metal door closed loudly behind them; a sinewy woman in a faded apron let them in, smiling and beckoning, speaking dialect. She crooned over Margaret, putting her hands on her, rubbing her upper arms vigorously, patting the bump in congratulations. Margaret looked over her shoulder to reassure David and wink. The woman gave them each an egg and a slice of brown bread, made them sit down at a rickety kitchen table, and deposited bowls of cracked black olives, dates and small cups of dark coffee before them. Margaret could feel the baby waking up inside her. She reached for David's hand over the table. It was clammy. He was trying to answer the woman's questions in his pock-marked Italian.

Childbirth. This screened sacrament. He saw his wife into a small room and left her there.

While Margaret laboured, he looked out at the desert.

When he came back, there was a whole other female animal, giving off her own smell, and his wife looking like an athlete laureate, recently oiled and changed into bright linens.

The baby when he met her was a shock. She was howling and a bit grey, ugly as a raw prawn. But when he scooped her up, able to hold her whole body in the span of one hand and cup her head in the other, she stilled. He clicked at her, random soothing sounds like a home appliance emitting a thrum into blank household hours, the way all of Ralph's children had enjoyed, and she stared at him with huge eyes. He stared back. Her small eggshell skull was matted with mousy fuzz. He smoothed it down and brought her to his nose. She smelled like cinnamon, buttered toast and milk, a bit like a very young dog. He took a close look at the skin of her face. He could see no pores on it.

She sounded in the deep of him; he felt it in his pelvis and the soles of his feet. Her tiny hand freed itself and came out waving, he lifted his finger and it came down over it. She blinked very slowly. Her mouth puckered and she let out a long, just-audible sigh. Her ear was up against his heart now, and he willed it to slow so that it wouldn't be too loud for her, taking deep breaths and holding them for a moment inside his lungs before releasing them. He brought her up to his face again and passed his mouth over the top of her head.

They named her Hilary: the middle term of an Oxford year, when students took refuge in misty-windowed pubs. A quality of light that he missed. An Oxford January. Its clarity. The way the sounds of bells travelled through it with swift ease. Georgian windows filling at sunrise. The high song of a chorister in candled dark. Gregorian mass as he had once heard it in Florence, in San Miniato al Monte at dusk, having just eaten lemon sorbet. Its deep dark of evenly spaced and painted stars.

He went into the room where his wife lay resting.

– Do you mind if we call her Hilary Ann?

They had previously agreed on Hilary. Joy. A good name for when you have blown up your life.

Margaret said yes.

It was so that he could send the telegram to his mother: 'Hilarious Announcement: –'

He never got a reply. Soon, his mother would have a series of strokes stacked close together, and die.

44

Their life will see them range over the world seeking a place where his work matters as much to him as it did before: Australia, Switzerland, West Germany, finally France. There will be times when they will stand across from one another in their kitchens and will barely be able to speak of it.

– Aren't you tired, my love?
– I gave it all up. For you.
– Don't say that. That's not true.
– Yes, it is.
– No, it's not. It wasn't just me.
– You were the one   who
– Please. Be fair.
– You have never acknowledged how much more I had to lose.
– Please.
– You had no family.
– That is true. I did not.
– Is it supposed to be like this?
– What do you mean?
– Marriage. You and me. So . . . lonely, sometimes.
– Our circumstances are somewhat specific.

– I miss it.
– I know you do.
– If you had your time again?
– I think I would have been gentler with you.

It was 1984 and he wanted to move again. To the South of France this time. She scoffed at him, the arch laugh she reserved for moments when she needed him angered from the off. There were no roads! The ones they did have were lined with plane trees. When you travelled along them, they made you feel like you were zooming into a postcard. Is that what he wanted? Some romantic postcard life, in a remote place where they knew no one, where he couldn't speak the language? Surely he wouldn't do that to her. Not again. Not now, when she was finally happy and settled, with friends.

– All our life I have followed you. Isn't it time we stood still?

– Margaret. Please. I can't stand another winter in this place.

The new house had room for them to sleep separately, so they did. It was an almost wordless transition. They just moved in and split the sets of bedding.

Hilary was at university then, and they were left alone in what remained. They had to figure it out anew. Someone in the village told them of a stretch of the river only accessible on foot. It was in the gorge, close to the source, you could see the water coursing out from under the rock.

They parked the car under the shade of the plane trees by the mairie. They began the climb up the rough white stone path. They were having a row about how he'd brought them here, bought a house with no central heating, and didn't speak the language. The argument dilated and billowed as they came to the top of the rise and began their descent. They would both remember the details of its hurts, how their words moved over the stones. The path was steep, with jutting roots. Wild rosemary sent up its starry strands. Quatrefoil cistus, white and pink, moved under the weights of enormous opalescent black bees. There was a single breeding pair of eagles in this place, they'd been told. David kept watch for them.

They emerged at the bottom of the gorge, on a carved bank. The river was clear. Schools of small trout swam in it. The cicadas, of course, kept up their liebestod. Blue and white and tiger-striped butterflies moved erratically over the scene. The row broke off, foundered on the beauty before them. Margaret reached for his hand.

– Pax?

He smoothed his thumb through her palm.

– Pax.

They walked to the water's edge, where a sapling poplar clung to a gap in the rock and cast a speckled shade. David began to undress, and she followed. She was stilled once more by the beauty of his legs. She loved them so. She remembered how she had always desired him, from that moment he had appeared to her beneath the spreading cedar; but she did not love him until after they'd been parted: those long nights in the phone booth, when he began to shed his steadfast certainties. He was in his sixties now, and the skin over his muscles had loosened, had come away a little. She was the same, she knew. She stepped out of her underwear and left her clothes piled on her towel.

They stood before one another. It was her frankness that he loved, which had always drawn him to her. Her cleavage was carved with heavy lines now, but he loved it when she pulled it into a bra and wore a printed wrap dress. It said, this is my body, and it has been in the sun at every opportunity of its life. This frankness was so incredibly sexy, the most attractive thing about her. She was a beautiful woman who spoke plainly, and he had never known another like her. She stood before him now with their history visible upon her: the stripes that ran over her where she accommodated their child, the nipples, a jagged edge of scar on her shin.

She hung back to watch him dive, as she had long loved to do. Here he was at ease with himself, and to see it was the deepest of her pleasures.

She joined him. They trod water with each other. She brought her legs up round his waist. Her thighbones made the shape of a yoke around him, and he smiled and felt the smile spread all along his shoulders. The first time she ever put her legs around him, bringing both of her thighs flush with his ribs and locking her ankles one against the other, it had been a shock. He had gasped at how good it felt to be so braced. He came quickly then, and afterwards she laughed gently at him (tracing the shelf of his shoulder blade). Now he brought his hands up and smoothed them over her breasts, as he had learnt to do by then. So long ago. They placed their hands on the backs of one another's heads. The taste of her, in the curve of her neck, was the same as it had ever been. They retired to the shade and moved in it in their well-worn way.

✤

Another time, another place. She says: – It is good. Here, with you.

He spreads his arms and grins at her, and birds climb in the currents of the air as he replies: – Let me lessen my request. Let me breathe between the heavens and the earth, a private man.

To live a quiet life: this too can be a radical political act.

45

In London, Adrian cycles to and from work. Everywhere are being laid the bones of new buildings. They send their lift shafts into the sky first. The noise of these works is a great commotion. His bicycle ticks beneath him. Now and again he thinks of her: he likes to picture her on the balcony after the morning sun has passed, the valley beneath her, intermittently asleep. He hopes for a gentle breeze upon her face.

— Mama?

It is what he calls her when he is trying to cajole her. Hilary is gardening. Midnight in London, four p.m. in California. – Darling? she says, and sits back on her knees. There is a hummingbird dancing with the cardinal blooms of the salvia.

— I think you should be proud. To be descended from such a marriage.

He has used the grand words to make her laugh, and she does, and then her vision is swimming with tears. She smiles, and the sobs slide out of her like something shucked, and higher up the hill, beyond the houses, the mountain lions walk on padded paws.

But all this is yet to come. In another now, it is the hot night. Dry winds blow and sand stings the panes of windows. There is the occasional bark of a dog or call of some more liminal animal. A husband is his most unabashed now. His wife may lie propped in the bed in the grey light, feeding their baby, looking at him.

My pearl, he calls her. My pearl of great price. My pearl beyond pocket.

The light is taking its last leave of the evening. There are two people who have not drawn their curtains yet. Through a large square window, they can be seen: a man and a woman, living, we might suppose, in the manner in which they have been told they ought. In the warmth of the lamps, they reach for each other.

It is not long after dawn. A man walks in the warming sea with his baby in his arms. He holds her to the sun. She kicks.

Author's Note

My grandfather was a Catholic priest. My grandmother was a laywoman. He died of cancer when I was six. She died in 2023, having had dementia for three years.

There is a single folder remaining from my grandfather's time as a priest. It contains typed and handwritten lectures (or sermons?) he gave, and one written by her. I have quoted these, sometimes interweaving or editing them, in this book.

The 'Parable' on page 229 is from an undated document in that same folder – I don't know which of them wrote it.

My great-uncle really did say that to Archbishop Dwyer.

My grandmother really did tell a senior member of the clergy that the Old Mother Church was a bitch.

In my research, Xavier Rynne's *Letters from Vatican City*, both the article series he wrote for *The New Yorker* between 1962 and 1965, and one of the resulting books of the same title (Faber and Faber, London, 1963), were invaluable in making the internecine debates of the Second Vatican Council intelligible to me. I also benefited greatly from reading Peter Manseau's *Vows: The Story of a Priest, A Nun, and their Son* (Free Press, New York, 2005), Claire Henderson Davis's *After the Church: Divine Encounter in a Sexual Age* (Canterbury

AUTHOR'S NOTE

Press, London, 2007), Charles Davis's *A Question of Conscience* (Hodder & Stoughton, London, 1967), Anthony Kenny's *A Path from Rome* (Sidgwick & Jackson, 1985) and Thomas Keneally's *Crimes of the Father* (Sceptre, London, 2016). Early inspiration came from Timothy Egan's description of his own Catholicity, 'lapsed but listening', in his book *A Pilgrimage to Eternity: From Canterbury to Rome in Search of a Faith* (Viking, 2019).

The phrase 'pearl beyond pocket' on page 270 is a quotation from Simon Armitage's translation of *Sir Gawain and the Green Knight*.

The passage 'There are hopes growing [...] Passion is only one mode of love' is inspired by John Berger, in his essay on seeing the Grünewald Crucifixion again after ten years, first in 1963 and then again in 1973. It can be found in *Portraits: John Berger on Artists*, edited by Tom Overton (Verso, 2015), '9. Matthias Grünewald (c. 1470–1528)', pp. 49–56.

The line 'the limit of our sight' is borrowed from Rossiter Worthington Raymond ('Life is eternal; and love is immortal; and death is only a horizon; and a horizon is nothing save the limit of our sight.')

The line 'Let me lessen my request . . . a private man' is adapted from William Shakespeare's *Antony and Cleopatra*.

Wendell Berry writes that God's instructions for humanity with regards to Creation can be boiled down to two words from Genesis: 'keep it'. Giovanni's comment echoes this. (*The World-Ending Fire: The Essential Wendell Berry*, Penguin 2017.)

The late-night news clipping in which Adrian learns about Regina Mundi and its closure is excerpted from an article written by J. Allen, Vatican correspondent for *The*

AUTHOR'S NOTE

National Catholic Reporter, on June 17, 2005: https://www.nationalcatholicreporter.org/word/word061705.htm#eight

'It matters not how strait the gate [...] captain of my soul' is a quotation from the poem 'Invictus' by William Ernest Henley. The conclusion which David draws from it – that we are not, after all, masters of our fate, but that we can try to be captains of our souls – is inspired by the graduation speech my mother gave to the IB graduating class of 2013 at L'Ermitage, Maisons-Laffitte.

The line 'I am Jezebel of ill renown/who met death wearing her crown' is taken from a pamphlet I found in my grandmother's papers, *Celebrating Women*, 1987, Janet Crawford and Erice Webb, 'A Litany for Many Voices'.

Margaret's lesson about Luke 1:34–35 (Douay-Rheims), is inspired by Marina Warner, *Alone of All her Sex: The Myth and Cult of the Virgin Mary* (Picador, London, 1985, p. 36).

'To be descended from such a union' is from L. P. Hartley's *The Go-Between*.

Acknowledgements

Thank you to my agent, Matthew Marland, for all his attention and support, and all at RCW, especially Sam Coates and the rest of the foreign rights team. I am deeply grateful to my editors: in particular Anne Meadows, for her deep and immediate understanding of this book; Orla King, Elisabeth Schmitz and Laura Schmitt; and Sabine Erbrich, for her early enthusiasm for the manuscript. It has been a privilege and a joy working with so many brilliant women. Thank you to all at Picador, Grove Atlantic and Suhrkamp.

Thank you to my students at the Lycée International Winston Churchill, with whom reading *Antony and Cleopatra* was a revelation. I hope my students at Colfe's will enjoy it too. Thank you to my colleagues at both.

Thank you to sculptor and stonemason Edgar Ward, a man of enormous and exciting talent, for letting me spend the day in his studio and ask him about City & Guilds. Hugo Sharp, who came to our aid when our need was great: you are a treasure.

Thank you Father John Flynn, Professor Maurice Whitehead, Sister Mary Joseph, and Martin at the Venerable English College in Rome, for being so generous in their time

ACKNOWLEDGEMENTS

in corresponding with me and for the tour. Thank you to Professor Diarmaid MacCulloch for his very helpful suggested reading.

Thank you to the Society of Authors and the Hartsop Residency; to Milena Williamson, Hartsop neighbour, and her husband Eoghan for their elucidating insights into my thinking for this novel. Thank you again to the Society of Authors and its judges, for granting me a Somerset Maugham Award, which allowed me to travel to Rome. Thank you to Shaun McDowell for the residency at Torri in Sabina, and my godparents Andrew and Fiona, in whose house much of this book was edited.

Thank you again to all my teachers, past and present, but, perhaps most pertinently for this book: David Felton and Diana Francis, who taught me history of art at A-Level.

Thank you to my Lola for always being on hand to answer questions about Catholicism; to my first editor, Rachael Allen, for her friendship and encouragement; to Sandeep Parmar for witty bitching on the Heath. Thank you, T, for the love which was like driving in the dark. To my friends, loves of my life.

I would like to express my profound thanks to all those who cared for my nana at the long end of her days: Mary O'Brien and all at Présence 30, Dr Lalloyer, Samia, François, Adrien and Bénédicte, and all their colleagues, at MARPA Le Moulin in Castillon du Gard and, later, the Terrasses de Gisfort in Uzès. To Nana's friends, Joan Scott-Davis and the rest of Nana's bookclub; Nanni, Daniel Tommasi Kliwitsky and his dogs, whom Nana adored. To Gung George (no longer with us) and Nana Helen (still thriving), and the 'rest of the clan'.

ACKNOWLEDGEMENTS

Thank you to my brother and sister, for the bicycle, and many other things besides.

To my mother and her mother – formidable women, femmes formidables – thank you for not suffering fools gladly.